CORPSE SONG

A story of friendship, murder and betrayal.

Scott Dunlop

Big Squid Press

CONTENTS

PROLOGUE

"She rests upon the water,

Hair rising on one side.

Swans circling around her,

Dancing with their wide-eyed bride.

Willows weep upon the water,

Fish slide through the cold, dark lake.

Her beauty cannot be disturbed,

Weeds trail in her wake".

- Corpse Song -

Quiet country lanes flashing by; the sound of weeds lashing the sides of the car drowned out by the grinding of gears as deadly corners force me to slow down. Driving over the hill towards a homicidal maniac's hideout hadn't been part of the plan when I'd woken up that morning, but it was the only course of action that made any sense. For five of us, our entire lives had led to this point, the need to slam shut the door to the bewildering confusion that had cornered us. This mad race towards potential destruction could be the conclusion to an unfathomable evil that had somehow gained a foothold.

I couldn't tell you what music I had on the sound system, the rush of desperation constricted my thinking: all I knew was that at the end of this road lay the devastating cause of our loss of innocence. Not all of us had survived, but there was a chance that those who remained could claw our way back to sanity.

I shoved my foot against the accelerator and my ancient car lurched into the unknown.

CHAPTER ONE

Finn's Sunday best - 1975

There's a large, wooded area on the lower slopes of the hills, covering the ground right down to the side of a lake. To one side of the lake is a small island with a cabin on it, a couple of boats bobbing against a pier that thrusts out into the water from a black-pebbled beach. It's raining, and clouds obscure the tops of the mountains in the distance.

Sunlight is striking through the grey swirls. I'm fifteen again, and everything is about to change.

***

God's fingers. That's what mum used to call them. To me, those beams of light seemed to be more like prison spotlights, out to catch vagabonds and miscreants. It was best to stay in the shadows when God's fingers were about, just to be on the safe side.

The religious side to my mother never sank in with me. She'd press on us the need for propriety, as if God had nothing better to do than to watch over children and their manners (or the lack of them). On Sundays, she'd smooth our hair back with her hand and wipe around our mouths with a tissue she'd kept rolled in her sleeve. She'd spit on it, and we'd scrunch our eyes up tight in horror as she scrubbed away any evidence that we weren't good enough for God's stern judgement that scanned the pews for sin. Our collared shirts threatened to strangle us, and our feet ached inside polished shoes. Worst of all, it was the only day of the week when most of the village would be together in one place, so if you wanted to people-watch, you had to do it through squinted eyes during prayers.

On the best Sundays, you could catch a glimpse of Amelia Pickering. Talk about the Fingers of God - she looked like she'd been touched and that the light had remained, radiating out of her with a purity that almost burned your eyes.

My older brothers would fidget, nudging each other in the ribs and cuffing each other across the ears - distracted until mum would fix them with a glare that could freeze orange juice.

Back then, the seasons came and went with comforting predictability. Spring arrived in the first two weeks of April, the days grew longer, and leaf buds emerged on naked branches. The last snow would shrink back up the slopes, while streams were smooth as they snaked through valleys down to the lake. Birds drifted back one by one or in languid flocks to sing the days into moments of promise.

We had no sense of distance - running up and down the slopes, scrambling up willows and oaks, building dams or hurtling after rabbits - we'd not stop moving until night fell and the call to return home would come for food that was eaten without complaint. Lithe, with a fitness not concerned with goals or targets, we'd just stay in motion.

Our lives revolved around the land that hemmed us in, a broad circle of hills around the lake, with only one main road in and out of town. A road used by vans that delivered goods to the few stores and occasional visitors to the sole hotel in town.

Both ends of the village were punctuated with pubs. One was more of a social club where weekend dancing and romancing was the order of the day while the other was a tougher place, where drunks could stare into their glasses all day long and arguments sometimes burst out onto the streets late at night. It was usually the girls who graduated to the pubs first, invited by older boyfriends looking to impress them. The romance of this was short-lived, as the boyfriends drank too much and lost any sense of being cool, lurching from bar to bathroom to throw up before trying to kiss their disgusted dates.

Dylan Williams – tall, imposing - turned out to be helpful in this regard. Never flirting with the girls, he'd just appear when the boys got out of hand, steering them outside with a firm fist like a blacksmith's hammer. You didn't say "no" to Dylan.

Rites of passage in this village that would see the young people leaving one by one for the temptations of the city.

The kids would ride circuits of the town on their bicycles, knowing which bumps in the road offered a chance to ramp and which stop streets could be ignored. Tennis balls jammed in their spokes, whirring down between the clinic and the general store, turning left just before the police station and up towards the school where there was a hole cut in the fence to the scuffed and worn football pitch. Oil stains marked the road outside the school, left by kids long since gone, driving away in their first cars - hand-me-downs with fatal leaks, clattering exhausts and rusted roofs.

Lakeside. A place where the two uniformed cops seldom had to deal with anything more than scuffles and disagreements between neighbours or teenagers smoking weed - unthinkable, really, that this place could become the host to a series of events that seemed primaeval in nature, reducing our existences to individual battles for life and death.

***

A few of us were just wandering around that day, not doing anything. Harry wasn't with us; he'd been ill for the past couple of days with some stomach bug, probably from eating unripe berries we'd found up above the reservoir. We'd ridden our bikes past his house but he hadn't even looked out the window when we whistled, so he wasn't himself. He was quieter than the rest of us, living inside his own head, always lost in thoughts that he didn't share.

It would have been Cotton Ball - his surname really was Ball, and he'd been called Cotton forever, Emery, Pete Fryer (older by a year or so) and me. Cotton wasn't your typical class clown; he was more than just a buffoon. He was able to draw the entire class into his antics, being a natural entertainer, able to adopt new personas at will. The teachers would often laugh too, despite themselves. He had mischief in his veins, a sharpness to his eyes that absorbed the mood of the room and transformed it. He wasn't ever entirely still, he had a lively restlessness to him that could be infectious, we'd gain an additional lift of energy when he was around.

Emery was more of an oddball, with an almost adult bluster, like a little old man masquerading as a child.

As the youngest of three siblings, I tended to defer to my friends, letting them set the agenda and finding a gap where I could fit in. Usually, we didn't have more than a few coins between us, but today we had a couple of notes, courtesy of two birthdays the month before and Pete's part-time work in the grocers. He did a delivery service, occasionally being allowed to drive the van for more distant runs, since he was already sixteen. His job also gave us access to cigarettes or rolling papers and tobacco which we'd pretend to enjoy, although it's hard to be suave and sophisticated when you're not smoking next to a roulette wheel in a casino, you're having to hide behind a barn so that you won't be spotted by your parent's friends and coughing into your elbow.

"Take a ride?" Pete was astride his bike, hands in pockets. He always looked like he was ready for it, no matter what *it* was. *Anything could happen*, was his preferred declaration.

Emery looked at his watch. He already knew what time it was, but he liked the affectation of a wrist glance. "Yes, but I can't stay for too long, we've got a meeting later". His parents spent most nights at a local home cell group for a church that had moved into town. They were the kind of family that you'd expect to see in a Dickensian novel - if you happened to peer through their window at Christmas, they'd all have been seated around a decorated table, most likely singing rounds of carols and wearing festive hats.

There's nothing wrong with a childhood like that, I just felt bad for Pete in comparison. He lived in a much smaller place with his mother; none of us knew where his father was. They didn't have relatives visit them, so maybe that contributed to Pete's natural gregariousness, an inherent need to be around people.

"Riders on the sto-o-orm", sang Cotton. He did that sometimes, speaking in lyrics or singing them out loud. "That's us, let's chase the wind!"

A bit dramatic, but that's how we were, having only recently left behind our true childhood in which we'd battled stretches of enemy forces (nettles) with broadswords (sticks) and gaped in awe at the bodies of creatures we'd find in the fields along with shotgun cartridges that showed someone had been around our territory. We lived close enough to farmland to be aware of the ebbs and flows of life.

We barely needed money for anything, we could go all day on fresh air and water from the well outside the church or straight from the stream that ran parallel to the main road. If the water was moving, it was okay to drink. At least, that's what we'd been told. Our parents knew we were self-sufficient and would make sure there was bread at home in case we got hungry, but we generally favoured staying outside over going home to eat.

There were few cars on the road, three parked outside the Town Hall. We knew the cars by sight, since the village was that small. That day, we scuffed our bikes to a stop as a red van we hadn't seen before drove slowly past us. It was big, so we couldn't even see through the driver's window, all we saw was a hand bopping in time to music against the window frame. Dark sunglasses on the guy's face, a black beard. A sticker on the back of the truck read "Fresh Lamb".

Pete observed the van's departure and made a languid

gesture with his arm. "No one's going to buy stale lamb, are they?". We laughed. He commanded a certain amount of attention wherever he went, as if he was a senior officer in the navy on shore leave, with his height and neat clothes. It was like hanging around with a young Gregory Peck.

We watched the man ease along the road until his brake lights vanished around the old oak that marked the turn into the petrol station, but didn't say anything to each other, just slid back onto our saddles and rode on in the opposite direction. It wasn't looking like rain that day, but you never knew for sure what the weather could bring in spring, so I was wearing a hooded top over a vest that had yellow stars printed on it in lines, like a strange inversion of a flag. My jeans were faded, tennis shoes scuffed, but only because that's what you did when you got new shoes, you took them for a ride along a dirt track to give them a bit of attitude as soon as you got them. I could see Pete leading the way, riding with his hands off the handlebars while Cotton pedalled furiously to keep up on a bike that he'd outgrown at least a year ago.

My bike had been my brother's mode of transport until recently. It still sported stickers all over it, pictures of the characters from the Battle for the Planet of the Apes film. Since it had been my older brother's bike, though, I was quite proud to be riding it; it gave me street cred.

Emery was lagging behind me, trying to get something out of a backpack he'd brought along, wheels wobbling as he tried to keep his balance. He was shouting something, but I couldn't catch every word. My guess was that we were aiming for the lake; Pete was guiding us.

We turned down towards the lake onto a track where a gate was sometimes closed, but not that day. You could go pretty much anywhere back then, there were no signs about trespassing, unless you got way up on the mountain near the old scout huts. Even the reservoir was open so you could jump in and swim for a bit before drying off on your back, watching birds wheel through the sky. That was way up before the ridge, though, so we preferred to head for the lake with its easy access to piers and a handful of rowing boats.

We knew who the boats belonged to - which ones we could borrow for an afternoon and which ones were off limits - so occasionally we'd haul our fishing gear out and pretend that we were in search of the Shark, an urban legend of a trout that supposedly weighed as much as a bulldog, but we were really just goofing off. Mostly, we'd find a few freshwater crabs and a couple of little flappers that we'd put right back. The real fishing happened elsewhere, where fresh streams poured down from mountains and hills in the surrounding countryside.

There was a row of boathouses to the left of the pier, all shuttered and locked, so we left our bikes leaning against them and walked in single file down to the water. At the edge, there was a short, sandy beach with banks of pebbles on either side. I picked one up, curled my finger around it and skimmed it onto the flat surface of the water. It didn't skip properly, it just skidded and sank into the water. Vegetation from the surrounding hills had made the water appear as black as coffee, although it was really brown if you cupped it into a clear bottle.

We spent a few minutes aiming our throws into the depths, but then a white shape caught my eye, slightly obscured by a burst of reeds. At first, I thought it was a swan, but those tended to stick to the other side of the lake where there was more vegetation. I showed the others.

"Probably a shopping bag", said Cotton.

Emery squinted. "A rock, maybe?" But we knew there were no rocks in that part of the lake.

Pete's height gave him an advantage as a lookout. "I think it's a dead dog", he suggested, and we shuddered. This was where we *swim*, so the thought of something that big just rotting there was revolting. The nearest boat to us happened to have oars tucked into the sides, so we jumped in, jeans rolled up, shoes discarded.

It's tricky to tell distance across the surface of the water, but it must have been about a hundred feet away. Two of us pulled the oars, and we sliced through the water. At once, we stopped rowing, but the boat continued to slide forward with dreadful slow-motion precision. It was clear what the white shape was. A curved, swollen torso, a shoulder blade glistening in the sun. The whiteness of it was like seeing freshly laundered sheets hanging out to dry. We could see marbled purple shades, too, where her body touched the surface of the water, and a mass of matted and dried hair.

And that's how it started. The beginning of the end.

CHAPTER TWO

The girl with the shell necklace

I t was a Saturday afternoon when we found the body. I stayed on the shore with Cotton and Emery while Pete hurtled away on his bike. Cotton was jittery, unable to stand still, turning in wild, manic circles, while Emery was covering his face. I think he was crying as I could hear him sniffing every so often.

My legs had stopped working, it was all I could do to stand, so I sat on the edge of the pier. Within fifteen minutes a local cop car skidded to a stop, I could see Pete's face between the seats. He was as pale as I'd ever seen him, but also gritting his jaw, perhaps to avoid shoing his emotions. The ambulance from the clinic was just a blink behind, and other cars just kept on coming. I couldn't stop staring at my feet, so I barely noticed as someone drew a blanket around me and led me away to an old station wagon, the kind with wood panels and brown, leather seats. It smelled like cherry tobacco; a wooden cross hanging from the rear-view mirror.

After that, it was a flurry of being transported around town: to the small hospital, just a clinic, really, then to the police station, where people asked us questions. Finally, at home. My bike was still down at the beach, but the idea of fetching it was overwhelming. My father had come home from work, although I have no idea who called him, and my mother's face was tense with worry. I was eating a beetroot sandwich, careful not to drip the purple vinegar onto the table or down my front.

"Finn?" Mum was talking into her hands, which were clenched in front of her mouth.

I looked at my parents. They stared back.

"You okay there? What you saw today, that's not something anyone should ever have to see." My dad looked more worried than I'd ever seen him.

The thing is, I guess I've seen worse things. A dead cat, seething with maggots around the side of the school. A cow that had died on the slopes above town, bloated and on its back in the grass, all four legs in the air like an inverted table. That time Emma Vickers threw up in class after eating strawberry ice cream and there was a foul, pink, mess. The hole in my knee after I jumped out of a sycamore tree and hit a nail jutting out of a fence pole. The body in the lake had only partially been visible, so it wasn't that bad to see. It was more the thought of how it could have got there that was unnerving.

"Finn?" I guessed they'd noticed my mind was wandering.

I was only a kid, but I could tell they were struggling with what to say. What can you say to a child who has seen something like that? I wondered what Pete, Cotton and Emery's parents were saying to them. Pete would probably have shrugged it off after the initial shock and would be acting as if he was fine. Cotton was more likely to be crying a bit, while Emery would be distracted, counting marbles or sanding a piece of wood into a smooth shape.

I wasn't sure what to say. I took another bite of my sandwich, then put it down, remembering the way the body in the water had purple marks on the shoulder, like beetroot stains.

"I'm fine". (I wasn't).

"Kiddo, just tell us if you need to talk about anything. We're right here for you".

They left the kitchen, went into the lounge, where I could hear them speaking in low tones. Looking around the doorframe, I told them I was heading out to get my bike. They nodded, knowing there would be plenty of people down at the beach and that I'd be safe.

***

It seemed like the whole town had downed tools for the day. Sure, it was a Saturday, but there were groups of people on every corner. In turn, they watched me as I passed and their conversation fell still. I wished I had my bike right then so I could pop a wheelie to show how nonchalant I was, but instead, every step I made in the dust felt like punctuation to their horror.

As I walked past Harry's place, I looked up, out of habit. His face was in the window, but then it looked like his mom drew the curtains right away. The fabric twitched and then settled. Already he'd been separated from the rest of us, the ones who'd seen what shouldn't be seen. Small towns have a way of dividing situations into groups. In the same way that some friends clotted together after school and others never spoke again, anyone who had been affected by some tragedy - the loss of a parent, for example - walked about with an invisible sign over their heads for a while until the next tragedy came along. My only allies right now were Pete, Cotton and Emery, and we were in that small-town spotlight.

All three of them were down at the lake. Their faces must have mirrored mine. They looked a bit shocked, quieter than usual and not buzzing with the strange energy that normally kept us on the move. Pete looked older, as if he'd aged in just a couple of hours. He'd lost any childlike qualities and had a grim set to his clenched jaw. He spoke without taking his eyes off the patch of reeds where we'd seen the body.

"How was it with the cops?" he asked. We filled him in - each of us had repeated the story, not that there was much to tell. "Yeah, same here," he said.

We sat in a line away from all the cars and people walking about with folders, equipment and torches. Someone was setting up large lights that created beams of yellow across the water. It would get dark soon, so I guessed that they'd want to keep on going into the night. The body was gone, and the boat we had used was being examined by two men, and the other boats had been closed off with yellow rope strung between poles. We could hear the fizz and crackle of two-way radios and murmurs of discussions between people as they moved about. The mood was what I understood to be funereal, although I'd only ever been to one funeral before, a relative who had passed away a couple of years previously. She'd always lived alone, coming to church now and then to peer over her hymnal at others in the congregation without saying much. Her funeral had been a serious, glum affair: a few men shifting from side to side in the pews and checking their watches and some older women who seemed grateful that it wasn't their turn just yet.

Invasive. I felt indignant that our spot next to the lake had become the stage for some lurid cop show drama. It was supposed to be a place where people could enjoy the scenery, explore the lake and unwind. I was angry, I suppose, and turned to my friends.

"You know what we have to do, right?"

They looked at me, uncertain.

"We have to fix this as quickly as possible so we can get our lake back".

"How the hell are we supposed to do that?" Cotton asked, "We're just useless, like prawns in chess."

It took me a moment before I understood what he'd said.

"It's pawns, idiot, and they can come in handy if you know your moves".

"Alright, we're as useless as a trifle without sherry in it".

That made more sense, since, as children, we all enjoyed the ridiculously sophisticated notion of having alcohol in our food at Christmas.

I meant it, too, about fixing things, only I had no idea how to go about it.

***

If you want to be a part of the social telephone, run errands for local businesses. Small tasks like dropping a package from one side of town to the other let you into places you wouldn't normally be. Better yet, you'd be somewhat invisible, just a kid with their bike, so conversations would stop for a beat and then carry on. You don't even need to ask questions, people just talk over your head. In a small town, this means you get a broad overview of everything that's happening over the course of one morning. I'd used the pretext of the unusual circumstances at the lake to offer my help to a few local business owners - *you're probably busy with the... thing... activity; need me to run an errand for you?* That gave them a few minutes to shoot the breeze with customers and other people who were coming and going, as well as letting me hear the lowdown.

After a couple of hours of this, I knew as much as anyone about what was going on:

A few kids had come across a body in the middle of the lake (that much, we knew). The body wasn't clothed. No one knew who it was. The coroner had been liaising with city cops and hospitals to see if there were any recently missing people. Well, women, at least. This was a woman, after all. Beyond that, the details also seemed to get blurred: the body had drowned (maybe). The person had been shot, stabbed or strangled (or a combination of these). It was a homicide. It was an accident or natural causes. Perhaps it was to do with drugs or some other form of crime. While people in town aimed for discretion in their conversation, I understood that when they referred to crime in this sense, they meant she might have been a prostitute, or sex worker as we would say now. Academically, I knew what that was, but it was a world beyond my frame of reference, and it would have been highly unusual if there were sex workers in our miniscule version of society in the village.

The biggest news was that while the body had no clothing, she was wearing a necklace. It was still around her neck, but her fingers were wrapped around it, too. I'd heard that by taking a break outside the police station and sitting on the grass against the wall to drink a soda. The window was open and Jarvis, one of the local cops, had quite a loud, nasal voice that carried above the sounds of the town. The cells (there were just two), were empty, creating a space for noise to be magnified, echoing off the concrete. A necklace made of a leather thong and strung with shells. Jarvis made an off-colour joke about calling the woman Shelley, but no one laughed with him.

Shelley. Despite myself, I thought of her as that, picturing a young woman down at the edge of the sea, impossibly beautiful, swirling the foam of the waves and the sand between her fingers, her eyes fixing on one bright shell after another. She was wearing a white, cotton dress overlaid with a work pinafore, a pocket on the front. Shelley had collected a handful of shells, kicked at the breakers and laughed, then headed back up to the walkway where her black shoes lay in the sun: very much alive.

It felt essential that we find out more about this woman and how she'd found her way into our lake in a valley surrounded by green hills. That we re-clothe her with her own story and restore her dignity as well as our place at the lake.

CHAPTER THREE

The world's a tumble dryer

The summer break stretched over several weeks, and we lost track of time. The weeks started to become months and it became clear that the flame ignited by the discovery of the body in the lake was flickering, struggling to stay lit. We still rode around on our bikes, but the sense of purpose we'd had of trying to solve the mystery waned and we found ourselves aimless again. If anything, the aimlessness was frustrating, since we wanted to resolve the drama.

Harry had joined us again once his illness had cleared up, but our little crew had lost some of its sparkle in town; it felt like we were tainted by the fact that we'd been the first to stumble upon the woman's body. Harry wanted all the details, but we had nothing more to offer him. None of us wanted to describe that bent, dead human we'd seen in the water.

Cotton had toughened up a bit over the break and had managed to add a couple of inches to his height. He wasn't as tall as Pete, but then Pete was always like one of those saplings that towers above the rest, as if racing to be the first to catch the dawn's rays. Emery had lost a bit of his puppy fat and was showing evidence of a beard. It was strange, since he was blond, so it looked like he'd just been drinking milk out of the bottle, leaving a ring of white around his mouth. I'd spent the past few weeks learning to play my brother's guitar in the garage at home but hadn't progressed much beyond three chords on the out-of-tune instrument.

We went back to school, grew tired of sharing the same narrative about what had happened that day. It was tempting to make up additions to the story - that we'd seen the shadow of a man on the far side of the lake, or that the woman's eyes had appeared to shine with a demonic light, but we knew that these embellishments could put us back in the police station being interviewed once more.

Summer shifted to autumn and winter followed too soon, a massive storm moving in brought with it rain that lasted for an entire week, pooling in the roads and keeping us indoors. The lake flooded, washing away some of the trees we'd known all of our lives. The elm, known locally as the Hanging Tree, with its outstretched arms and tyre-swing rope lay prone in the shallows. The willows still wept into the water, although the largest of them drowned with its roots immersed in water. Ice fringes began to appear on the surface of the lake as frost spangled the evergreens.

Just as suddenly, it was 1976.

***

In films, someone goes missing and the plot involves that person being found. The truth of it, as we would discover over the next few years, is that sometimes, a body is just an isolated thing; a full stop with no sentence. No matter what evidence exists, a person can vanish from their own existence and reappear as just a mass of flesh and bone with no identity. Sometimes they just walk out of their lives and are never seen again.

From what I could gather, her remains were kept for a long time before being buried in a corner of the churchyard under an unmarked stone. The police kept photographic evidence, but the body itself lacked any significant details and didn't need to be kept in a fridge in the morgue anymore. I guess there was a whole lot of paperwork involved in this process but I never saw any of that. All that would have been retained would be a file with photos of the lake scene and her body, some vials of blood, maybe, and that shell necklace, now dried and twisted into an envelope marked "evidence".

We had theories: she'd been a spy from some foreign agency who'd crossed the line and revealed her identity; she was an exchange student, brought from another country to learn clumsy English phrases while looking after someone's kids; she was a drug dealer who'd tried her own product and gone crazy, only to drown in the lake during a late-night swim - the theories got more and more insane - like, perhaps she was a time traveller who had set her machine coordinates incorrectly and, unable to swim, had fizzed into being in the middle of a lake.

Endless nights of meeting each other to discuss our theories with no evidence to go on. When we tried to eke information from the police, we were politely asked not to interfere, since the cops had it all under control. We knew that wasn't the case, and that the only thing they had control over were their custard cream biscuits they enjoyed over endless mugs of tea.

The theories didn't cover the possibility that she was a mother, a wife, a girlfriend or an employee. It was just too sad to imagine that a human being could be erased from an ordinary life with such anonymity and finality. As easily as a lost sock in a tumble dryer.

We pushed ahead with school; to us, leaving it behind was more important than whatever came next. The world felt like it was in limbo. More so, in our small village where the old men grumbled about mines closing and farmland shrinking. The city nearby was expanding, adding a couple of cinemas, a shopping mall of sorts and a football stadium that was occasionally used for rock concerts. Then we'd hear the bikers roll through the village in long lines of denim and leather, pausing to fill the pubs with their broad-shouldered virility and ridiculous handlebar moustaches. They'd roar away after a few pints, leaving the sheltered villagers shaking their heads in disapproval.

We spent more time travelling into town on weekends, getting lifts with older siblings or parents, trying to stretch our wings just a little bit at a time. From being content with our incremental village life, we wanted something bigger, as vague as that concept was to us.

***

I couldn't tell you exactly where the idea came from - we were just sitting around, talking nonsense - but at some point, on one of those rambling evenings we hit on the idea of starting a band. Maybe it was our graduation from village childhood to town adulthood that did it, with the realisation that clothes weren't just something we had to wear to avoid being naked or to keep warm, we could pose into action the attitudes we couldn't articulate.

"I mean, how hard can it be, right?" Pete had a point. "Bleedin' Bay City Rollers did it. Showaddywaddy did it. Anyone with a garage to practise in can get started". His point had lost its impact a bit with the two examples he'd chosen, both known for their posing and matching outfits, but each of us in turn pictured ourselves basking on stage. Glory. I suppose I wasn't alone in playing air guitar in front of the full-length mirror in my parent's bedroom.

After several months of playing guitar, I'd discovered the joy of power chords that I could slide up and down the neck to make a passable tune. Rhythm guitar. I've no idea how it happened, but Harry got a drum kit and turned out to be not too bad at keeping a beat, in his introverted, behind-the-scenes manner. Pete, in the way of lanky people, found that a deep red bass guitar picked up at a charity shop matched his style: when he walked, he had a rhythmic, loping step that converted well into those little bass runs that coiled like a spring into the tunes we were making. Emery was fairly musical, having had a piano at home all his life: the only one of us who could read music, and he shifted between lead guitar and keyboard with ease. Cotton was all wild hair and cheekbones, with an attitude that drifted between emotional vulnerability and endearing aggression: the perfect front man.

An introvert, an extrovert, a charmer, a player (a musical one, that is) and… me.

We scoured the thrift shops for something we could pass off as fashion, and, as 1976 became 1977, found that there was a new wave of music and style that seemed designed just for us. Towards the end of the year, after we'd all turned 18, we performed for the first time as The Impressions, a name truncated from "lasting impressions", which is what we hoped to leave. Our first gig was an amateur mix of edgy rock 'n roll and some more experimental songs that didn't find their audience.

The 70s had produced a zig-zag timeline in music that veered from technically complex prog rock to "everyone else is doing it, why can't we?". The Beatles had only broken up in 1970 when McCartney left, although the dissolution wasn't formalised until 1974, while the brief implosion that was the Sex Pistols started in 1975, lasting until early in 1978. Elvis was still performing in 1977 and even old timers like Frank Sinatra were still on stage. Punk in its many iterations had been birthed from proto punk and ended in post-punk and New Wave music, the latter being a careless blanket term for everything from the B52s to the Boomtown Rats or the Cure. Two Tone rubbed shoulders with dub and reggae, and anyone with a synthesiser was discovering the fast track to success.

The Impressions were New Wave before the term existed. We ignored the folksy, acoustic remnants that still remained from the 60s and leaned into the energy of punk with some pretty catchy melodies. It seems strange to recall, since those days are long gone, but we even managed to get a record deal and some local airplay for a few songs. One of them had nothing to do with Arthurian legend and romance, but listeners didn't know that. It was called "Lady in the Lake". It wasn't a good song, but it had plenty of adolescent dramatic energy.

Whenever we played it, I had to face the back of the stage,

unable to look out over the heads of the audience: I'd found that the shimmering effect of the spotlights made them seem like a pool of water, and more than once, I'd seen a formless, white shape tucked away in the corner of the hall. A woman's body, bobbing in time to Harry's drums.

There was something magical about being on stage, being someone else for a moment, not having to live with the past or the future, living out each second.

One memorable gig escalated from bad to worse with surprising ease. A heckler had been shouting at Cotton all evening, until Cotton had grabbed a crash cymbal and bashed him over the head. It was the only time I'd ever seen something approaching violence from Cotton, but even this action was more akin to slapstick comedy. Once the heckler had wobbled to his feet, he staggered outside to return with a gun, only it was a pellet gun. He chased us around the stage shooting tiny metal balls at our feet until Pete picked him up and locked him in the bathroom, where he'd passed out still holding a poster advertising the gig. He'd shown his dislike for the band in graphic style, streaking it with his own, awful, toilet-based signature.

The messy tours we cobbled together with Pete's help (he was great at convincing venue owners to let us in for a night or two) involved more debauchery than music. Cotton had a coterie of male and female fans who'd follow us from town to town, and Pete was able to home in on women, sometimes much older women, who were coyer than the younger ones but offering him the promise of experience. Emery and Harry tended to just hang out together, not too engaged with the madness of fame, while I preferred to chat to other musicians with whom we'd shared the bill, listening to their wild and embellished stories.

I found that the musicians who weren't embracing the absolute hedonism of it all were bored by the lifestyle. A common theme they shared was the desire to just be normal again. I agreed with them. It took immense energy to get up on stage to perform and then you needed to be careful when walking around to the shops or eating in a restaurant. I'd had friends who were attacked and beaten up by thugs who didn't like their image or music, as well as others who'd been snapped by photographers while looking worse for wear. The constant flash of cameras was mind-numbing, and I quickly understood why famous people wore shades all the time.

The band lasted a little over three years: not a bad run. Then Cotton, who had managed to pick up a regular drug and booze problem, got noticed by a bigger act whose singer had died in mysterious circumstances, adding to their notoriety. They'd needed someone to fill in, fast, and Cotton barely gave us a second thought before signing a deal with them. He thrived on being the centre of attention, of stripping down or dressing up for gigs, posing for pictures or goading TV presenters as they tried to interview him.

He'd got up one day during a rehearsal, mumbled "sorry, lads," and vanished into the night.

We weren't angry with him, since we'd never taken the whole industry ascension thing seriously. Pete moved away from the village to the nearest city where he got regular work as a session musician in recordings and supporting on tours, but mostly he helped out in a betting shop. The shop was a nasty little place, dark and dingy, with dodgy-looking punters coming and going. I wasn't entirely sure what a man like Pete would do there, except pose as a bouncer or coax people into bets they'd regret making.

Emery changed direction completely, gave up his half-hearted drug habit (which was really just a bit of weed on occasion). He declared himself "newborn" and spent his weekends playing in youth groups and in worship sessions in a small Christian-ish sect. Harry just packed his drums away in the garage and got a job in a small accounting firm. We'd almost forgotten about that awful day we'd found a corpse bobbing in the water. I got the call that my great aunt had left me something in her will, and that was the end of The Impressions, the end of the 70s and the end of our childhood.

CHAPTER FOUR

1995: Lightning strikes twice

The day the world changed for the second time; I was working in the book shop as usual. Unpacking some titles that I'd got at a steal from a publisher that was in trouble. They'd printed their usual quantities but then had a nasty realisation that the supply would outweigh the demand. After waiting a few months, they'd had to sell off stock to cover costs, so I'd snapped up a few boxes. Unpacking new books, cataloguing them into the store system and finding a home for them on the shelves is therapeutic. At first glance, there's nowhere else to put even more books on the shop floor, but a good bookseller knows how to magnify their space.

The store itself was picture-perfect, an ancient cottage situated at the part of town where locals and holiday makers would pass on foot on their way to the biggest supermarket in the area. It was pretty, so more people stopped to take photos than ever stepped inside, but I'd always preferred it when there were just a couple of customers at a time. That way you could have those strange, book-related conversations that were as intimate as a confession but limited to the magic that could be contained between two covers. The windows were small, so light couldn't damage the books on display, but there was life in the old building, life that seemed to emanate from the shelves, the solid, wooden counter covered in exactly the kind of curiosities you'd want to see in a quaint old bookshop to magnify the feel of a miniature world you could escape to for a half an hour.

I'd inherited the place about fifteen years previously, before I'd opted for any particular direction in life. A great aunt on my mother's side had died. I'd only met her a couple of times as a child; she'd been a strange, older person, with long, grey hair and hands that always seemed to be moving, as if she was knitting an imaginary blanket or one of the crocheted shawls she wore. Stranger still, she'd left this place to me by name in her will. It wasn't punctuated with any affectionate note, it was a simple request: T*he bookshop and its contents will pass to my nephew, Finn.*

At the time, I was adjusting to adult life and was at a bit of a loose end about the future. Studying didn't make sense, I was no academic, and I lacked the go-getter attitude you needed to head off to foreign places with a backpack. The arrival of a bookshop out of nowhere into my lack of purpose had worked out perfectly. I enjoyed reading and the store itself came with a challenge: trying to make sense of the system my aunt had in place, and then deciding to reimagine it all with a vision of my own.

The bequest had come with a small budget for maintenance, allowing me to make the alterations.

It was hard work: tearing down rickety shelves, putting up new ones, reorganising the books into sections and then alphabetising them and adding some ideas I thought would be exactly what I'd like to see in a quaint little bookshop.

It had nothing to do with the kinds of ambitions we're taught to have as children: start a business, grow a business, branch out with even more business and retire young. That wasn't me at all. I barely thought of it as a business at all. It just became who and where I was, as if it was a suit that had always been waiting for me to put it on.

I kept some of the older volumes along with a small collection of First and special editions in one corner so they could whisper their secrets to each other when I closed at night.

Space was a challenge, but the miracle of a bookstore is that there's always more room to be found. I didn't need to use the cellar for storage, but I didn't want to, anyway. It was dry, but it felt like the peat bog it had been built on over two hundred years prior was thirsty for fresh air and looking for a gap to emerge through the ancient stones.

This life wasn't a bad one. I got to work in a relaxing environment, taking holidays now and then. I had an assistant, Lucien, a quirky man in his thirties who wore the same off-purple beret every day. He didn't need full-time work and was happy to pop in and help out when I needed to get away or I just needed a bit of help. He was quite a reticent character, unless you got him talking about fantasy novels, his favourite genre. Lucien may not have played to the rules when it came to being normal, or, at least, in conversation, but he was reliable. When the mood took him, he surprised me with lucid wisdom that seemed to come from somewhere else inside his complicated mind.

***

Blacksea was the town closest to Lakeside, with an old market square that was home to a few shops - the fishmongers that also housed a fish-and-chips takeaway, a butcher, the new post office and stationers and a couple of small clothing stores selling unfashionable items. There were two schools and a sports centre, and a couple of churches, one traditional and one more modern, the latter meeting in the brick annexe to the Town Hall. There was an entertainment centre that showed films in a decrepit old cinema, but most residents headed to the city for the latest releases.

If someone recommends you read a book that you enjoy, it feels that they know you. The ones who weren't readers barely noticed me in the streets outside the shop. Reading provides a tier of anonymity - if you sit in a restaurant reading a book, the waiters and patrons start to treat you as if you're invisible. That works on public transport, too: in the city, if you have your nose in a book while riding the bus or the train, people are less likely to try and engage you in conversation. An introvert's armour.

It's easy for your past to vanish when you're living like that, from day to day, so I'd almost, but not quite, forgotten the time when, twenty years before, my world had changed for the first time. As much as I hate to reflect on that, it's a necessary task every couple of years to let those memories float to the surface.

The funny thing about memories is that they live in a world suspended in time. Children haven't grown up, the dead live and even cats and dogs that have long since been buried tearfully in gardens are loping happily about.

They say you can't read words in your dreams, but in memories, words slide in and out like driftwood tossed against a beach. Just as you think you have them in your grasp, they slip away, leaving only dragged hollows and formless echoes.

My memories may not be as intact as I'd like them to be, but it's important to record everything before the mists descend from the hills to cover everything completely, finally.

CHAPTER FIVE

What's in the basement?

I tend to treat life as a series of projects. Some never get finished, like the gardening tasks I'd set myself every year, only to give up as the seasons raced on ahead. Still, I meant to make the most out of the bookshop, even if the customers weren't purchasing as much as I'd hoped for. The biggest challenge was making the most out of the space. My living quarters were upstairs, with a large, single room covering the extent of the building. It was a converted attic, with a kitchenette on one side and a bathroom enclosed on the other. A lounge area was separated from the bedroom by an old wood and silk screen covered in paintings. It was homely, but I'd hoped that I could create a kitchen and dining room area downstairs in the cellar, maybe with a corner library. A personal library, even though I essentially lived in a bookshop, made complete sense to me.

That grand vision had seen me stripping away decades of junk in the cellar over the past few months. The flooring wasn't ideal: it was cold stone. I wanted to put in some wood flooring but would need to even out the surface and seal it first.

In the far corner, I'd started tearing up the original

stone, piling the slate slabs neatly to one side. As the project had progressed, I realised that a combination of stone and wood would look much better. The main problem was that the exposed area seemed to be way too damp.

I'd read a few books about the region after moving here in an effort to fast track settling in with the locals. The bookshop was built on an ancient peat bog that had, presumably, dried up enough for the original builders to deem it safe to build on. Way back in the day, peat would have been a major source of fuel for families living in the area, for whom the forests were out of bounds. The slabs of peat would have provided smoky warmth throughout winter, slow heat released by the rich remnants of rich vegetation.

My concern was that where there had been a bog, nature may try to move in once more. If I knew then what I know now, that would have been the least of my worries. In fact, I'd never have dug anything up, ever.

As it was, in some awful mocking repetition of history, I'd gone downstairs to work on the flooring. I was using the overhead lighting, but it was still fairly dim down there. As I crouched on the floor, deciding what to do next, I saw something. As much as I wanted to think I didn't know what it was, I knew, immediately.

In the corner where I'd upset the ground. It was dark and smooth, shiny as a polished chestnut and the same deep brown. Unmistakable. It was a bone. Or, at least, a shoulder. The soil tumbled away in dark clods and the curved dome of a skull appeared.

"Oh no. Actually, oh shit." I talk to myself quite a bit. I find myself a great conversationalist. I'd had a cat for a while, but she was never mine. She weaved her way into the house out of the shadows and made me feed her with her wide, green stare. We'd chatted quite a bit, me and TS (named after Eliot, but pronounced to rhyme with psst), until one day she'd wandered off into the shadows again.

Some people go through their entire lives never having

seen a body, even a relative's body. I couldn't quite wrap my head around that after all this time I was about to endure the same maddening cycle of activity that I had years before. As a child, the implosion caused by that first discovery had fed on itself like some greedy chemical reaction. The flames just rolled in on themselves, a roiling crater of magma that spewed lava bombs, smoke and toxic gases.

There were some immediate differences to this latest discovery, however: I wasn't a child anymore, I knew with relative certainty that no one had been in my cellar for a long time and then I also knew that the body wasn't fresh. It wasn't rotting, either, it was just... there. There was no foul stench, just the rich smell of the earth.

I could picture their faces: Pete, Cotton, Emery. I was imagining them peering out at this corpse from over my shoulder, ready to dash back to their bicycles and safety. In some ways, I wished for it. Twenty years ago, we'd all been in it together, even though we viewed it with different perspectives. I was standing in my own cellar, alone, with a body.

It was still morning, so I went back upstairs to my room, put the kettle on. Since it was a Sunday, I had the place to myself and the shop was closed. I thought about Aunt Freya, how she'd lived here for so long, no idea that she was in some form of cemetery, but then I realised that everyone is, to some degree. There's no permanence to death: burial grounds are sacred only for a short time before another generation will see the value in the land for redevelopment. The dead will be uncovered with a violence that no amount of prayers and consecration can undo. Bones will be gathered and reburied in a much smaller place, marked by memorial plaques rather than gravestones with writing that has long since succumbed to the elements. I'd read stories in the news almost every day of archaeologists and palaeontologists being called in as consultants on property developments when traces of humans were discovered. Students and academics would explore these sites under tents and tarpaulins for a few months before building would resume.

This was as true in this part of the world as it was in others, where shards of pottery and sharpened bone needles teased at civilisations long gone, and bones hinted at silent stories the world over.

That's just part of life, but the idea that my own home could become the next doctoral thesis for a would-be scientist wasn't sitting well with me. The local newspaper, starved for any real news, would probably print lurid and fantastic speculations about the origins of the human remains in my house, taking care to add a blurry picture of me emerging from my front door as if I'm a contemporary John Christie or Dennis Nilsen, a murdered with drains stuffed with body parts. Worse yet, a half-way decent journalist might uncover the link to the body in the lake of my childhood, feeding headlines like *"Lighting Strikes Twice In Mystery Corpse Case"*. If I'd opted to be a journalist instead of a bookshop proprietor, though, I'd probably have used exactly that headline.

Sitting drinking bad coffee doesn't help problems go away, however. It just adds to them (*"Corpse Finder Drinks Coffee Before Reporting Discovery To Cops"*?), so in the end I had to get up, and head to the police station to report what had happened. I couldn't face the idea of calling on the phone and trying to explain to the operator what had happened. At least a cop would see by my demeanour that I wasn't a threat.

***

It was raining outside - I hadn't noticed that since it had been sunny the first thing that morning - and I trudged the 200 metres or so to the police station with my coat wrapped around me. I looked at the houses on either side that were about to have their peace and quiet disturbed and nodded a silent apology at each one.

I felt an irrational guilt, the guilt that some people feel when they see a police van cruising past, as if I'd committed a crime and forgotten about it and only they knew.

Just before I pulled the door open to the police station, I looked at my feet. Screwed my eyes up as tightly as I could and, if "*please, please, please*" could be described as such, said a prayer to myself.

"Afternoon".

"Afternoon, Sir".

"I'm from the bookshop down the road. I need to report that I've found, uh, discovered, uh, a body. A dead body."

The policeman looked at me, his face undertaking a visible transformation from friendly village copper to *oh-my-god-this-is-my-time-to-shine* in the space of three seconds.

That's how long it takes for someone's life to change. Again.

CHAPTER SIX

A barrel of laughs

I forget to speak things out loud. I say them in my head, that's for sure, but then I see people looking at my face in askance and realise that I've not said a syllable. That's unless I'm on my own, in which case, I chat to myself non-stop.

So, there I was, with this policeman. He was blinking at me as if with every dash of his eyelids, another conflicting thought is crossing his mind. I watched his eyes move to his belt: an empty space where his truncheon would normally be. If I'd been an actual homicidal maniac, there's not a lot he could have done to keep me at bay, so I smiled at him in reassurance. (*"Smiling Killer Terrorises Brave Policeman"*). He backed up two steps and, through closed lips, called for help through the half door that separated the front desk from the back office.

"Sarge, could you come here for a sec, please".

A moment later, a woman appeared. She was quite square in the way she was built, angled shoulders, neat hat and immaculate uniform. I guessed that the uniform was telling untruths about her real figure, which I imagined would be slim and athletic. Her face was heart-shaped, her skin a bronzed

Mediterranean shade.

She was flexing her knuckles as if warming up for a fight. Despite myself, the context of it, I liked the way she was entirely focused on me.

"This gentleman says he's here to report a body. In his house."

I felt the need to interject.

"It looks like a very *old* body, and I didn't put it there. Can someone come and take a look, please?"

The sergeant didn't reply, she sized me up, appraising whether or not I presented any kind of danger. Finally, she said "Constable, we need a few 'someones', please".

That someone turned out to be almost the entire police squad, some of whom followed behind me as I walked back to the shop while others squeezed into two cars that raced ahead and then waited for me to catch up.

I opened the front door to the shop and let them file in. With all the books, there wasn't a lot of space, so I had to reach over their heads to point out the door down to the cellar.

"It's down there, in the far right-hand corner." As if I was directing them to a buffet table.

Two cops stayed upstairs with me. It was clear they'd been instructed to do just that, one on either side of me in case I needed to be apprehended.

There were some noises from the cellar and what sounded like several people swearing at the same time. Ah, I thought, they've found it.

It was a wretched situation. A single man living in an old cottage doing some digging in his own cellar, (for reasons he couldn't quite explain without it sounding more and more suspicious) finding a body. (*"Cellar Ghoul Exposed"*). This kind of story is exactly the sort of tale an amateur criminal would make up if they thought they could outsmart the law: just tell them there's a body and pretend you don't know how it got there. That'll fool 'em.

You can't really prepare for this sort of thing, unless, of

course, you've been through it before. Out of all the people in that room, I was probably the only one who had been in the presence of a mysterious corpse before, only this one wasn't in a lake. The detective in me was second-guessing my thoughts "you can't say for sure that it's *never* been in a lake, can you?".

I knew more or less what would follow, so I spoke to the sergeant in charge.

"I'm sure you'd like to chat to me at the station, can I bring a couple of things so I can check into the Inn afterwards? I reckon you'll be in and out of my cellar for a day or two." The day or two would turn into a week or two, but I'd guessed correctly.

She agreed, I got into the car as directed and was driven two hundred metres back up the road to the police station.

I sat in the interview room.

Over the next half an hour, I explained how I'd been living in the house for fifteen years and that I'd recently decided to remodel the basement. I couldn't decide which word sounded less like a serial killer: cellar or basement. Basement sounded more homely, so I went with that, although a cellar could be there to keep wine, so that was also potentially sophisticated.

Steeling myself, aware that even a perfunctory search of my childhood village would uncover my association with an old cold case, I decided to offer that in advance.

"You'll be amazed that when I was a child, over in Lakeside, I was part of a group of boys who discovered a body. Just a random body, they never found out who she was and how she found her way to the middle of the lake. So this isn't my first rodeo".

I was the one feeling amazed that I could distil that entire horrendous experience into a couple of dismissive sentences.

"You see, I'm no stranger to bodies, in case you're wondering why I'm not hysterical about it, but also, from what I could see, it was an ancient corpse, it looked mummified".

What I could see, though, was their faces drop in horror. This wasn't a big town, so it was likely that they didn't come across cellar bodies very often. I resolved to shut the hell up;

every sentence I'd said sounded like the guilty blurtings of a man caught in the middle of a crime. There's something to be said for saying nothing until you have your legal counsel present.

Another hour or so passed before someone knocked on the door, spoke in a hushed voice to the sergeant.

"Well, Mr Jones, it seems that there's no immediate cause for alarm, you're free to go right now, but please stay nearby. You mentioned the inn?"

I had, so I said I'd be checking in while they did whatever forensic tests they needed to do.

The Primrose Inn was in a building at least as old as my house, with rooms that weren't as roomy. It smelled like old beer and woodsmoke. Every conceivable surface had been covered in red fabric with what looked like a faded paisley pattern on it. Chairs, walls - even the door panels had this padded cell of an interior design motif going on.

For absolutely no reason at all that I could fathom, there were prints of pig paintings along the corridors and in my room. Beady-eyed porkers that looked like they had cameras installed in their eyes. I threw my bag on the bed and lay down. The bedlinen was a floral fabric that clashed horribly with the red paisley. A small window looked out on the main street; if I pushed my face against the glass I could almost see the book shop and my house, but then everything was nearby.

There was a phone next to me, and, on autopilot, I picked up the receiver and dialled a number I thought I'd forgotten.

"Pete? Yeah, it's me, Finn. Yes, *that* Finn. Not too bad, thanks. Actually, I was wondering if we could get together for a drink or a coffee, if you prefer. Tomorrow?" I gave a brief rundown of what I'd been through. He agreed.

"Perfect. I'm at Primrose Inn in Blacksea, near the shop. You can't miss it. See you at half five." I hadn't spoken to him for a long time. Our intermittent calls were held together by nostalgia and not much else.

I was shaking. One by one, I called them all, their numbers written on my mind as if burned in place by our shared history.

Harry was easy - he was still in the same place where he'd lived all his life. It was almost as simple as throwing a pebble at his window. Emery was happy to oblige; he'd made it clear that he hoped to be used by some spiritual force in a grand conversion story for all of us, so he must've seen it as an opportunity. Cotton was harder to find. I had to call his manager, then a friend of a friend and finally, a number where I had to ask for Holden Caulfield. I knew that was Cotton, since he'd been obsessed with the Catcher In the Rye at school and, later when John Lennon was gunned down, the link the killer had made to this book. Cotton admitted to using pseudonyms when he was at home so that he, too, could avoid fans and their weird ways of demonstrating their love for him. He'd had a stalker for a time who would send him clippings of their hair and ask him to do the same.

It was a quirk of fate that all of them were around after so many years and able to meet me at the inn on short notice. I half expected them to arrive on their chopper bicycles with sunburned noses and scuffed tennis shoes, daring me to jump off the pier and into the cold waters of the lake.

I hadn't packed much for my stay, so I just went to sleep in the same t-shirt I'd been wearing all day while being a handyman, a Ramones band shirt. I was allowed to wear the shirt because I was able to list far more than five songs, so I tried to do just that, in order of release, so I could calm my mind and get some sleep. I guess I fell asleep somewhere between *Pet Sematary* and *Poison Heart*.

When I looked out the window the next morning, I could see a couple of white vans and a car with cop lights on top were parked outside my house. It looked like the front door had police tape around it, too. There were a lot of people walking around, considering it was a Monday, so I guess some of the details had been whispered around town. Coffee. It was a need more than a want. Downstairs, I grabbed a mug from the breakfast corner and went outside. A woman who'd recently bought a copy of a Jeffrey Archer novel from me caught my eye. She was walking with her child. She lowered her gaze and crossed over the street without greeting, leaving me with a stupid smile on my face staring at the space she'd just left.

There are two reactions to horror, especially real-life horror. The human fascination for it can attract some people, who want to get up close, rub shoulders with death; maybe as an acknowledgement of their own mortality and the absurdity of it. The other reaction is to blot it out, like families who never visit sick relatives in hospital, or children covering their ears with their hands and shouting "I can't hear you!" when faced with something they don't want to confront. My predicament as the man with the body in the cellar had just set me apart for the second time in my life, and it was unsettling.

Decent people would maintain their polite facade with me, which was okay, since I knew how to do that too, working in retail. It stung, though, when you wanted more from a conversation and excuses were made. Bad excuses that were clearly false and they know that you knew what they were doing.

"Well, I'd better get going, I've got dinner to start/something to pick up/things to do/always busy - life never stops, hahaha."

I wasn't laughing. I wasn't sure what was happening, but I could see it was going to have long-term repercussions. Worse, still, my mind betrayed me, and I started humming the worst possible earworm: Lady in the Lake. The Corpse Song. Today was going to be a mess, and it had barely started.

I'd asked the manager at the inn if I could reserve a small room off the bar. It was technically a library, but I know from experience that it was a place where card games with low bet limits took place some weekends. Quiet, discreet. Right around the time that the band had split up, I'd stopped drinking, it just didn't make sense without the social element, and the social element that I'd encountered had leaned heavily towards drugs, too. I didn't miss it, even if the town's main events revolved around people swigging back endless quantities of beer. I was happy to head upstairs and get stuck into a book at night and even happier to wake up with a clear mind the following morning. When I'd been a drinker, I tended to get drunk just because I was absent minded about it: if the bottle was next to me, I'd not realise I was topping up until it was gone, along with my ability to balance.

There was a small honour bar in the room I'd reserved, so I'm sure the manager had made a note of what was in the fridge. They'd offered to keep a few jugs of ale and water coming, too.

Emery was first to arrive. He looked like he'd just stepped out of the shower, and he had a disconcerting suntan. Throwing back his arms expansively, he drew me into a massive hug. He had a bit of a belly filling out his pale, grey suit, but then none of us were getting younger.

"Finn! What a great surprise! You look good, man, you look fantastic". I thought I looked a bit haggard after my night in the inn, but he was always polite.

Inexplicably, he had a faint American accent. Perhaps it came from listening to too many sermons on audio cassettes. It certainly made for smoother prayers and encouragements to tithe, unlike the local accent, which could be jarring, containing a few words that outsiders wouldn't have understood.

He filled me in on the past few years, said he was the chairperson of a small organisation specialising in personal development, using the latest in motivational technologies (he called them that) to help people achieve their full potential. I asked him how lucrative that kind of business was, and he smiled a crocodile grin of capped teeth. He didn't mean it to be, but it was menacing. He suggested that he had more than enough and a stash or two offshore, just in case.

We kidded about, chatting more about what we could have been up to if we'd stayed together as a band, even if that had never been an option. He said he still composed music, but he did soundtracks, preferring the anonymity scores provided. He said he used a different name for that, something to do with his tax structure.

Harry entered the room, looking, well, harried. He shook

hands in a perfunctory way before sitting down in a corner seat as if he was hiding behind a snare and a hi-hat. He just blended into the room as if he'd been sitting there all along. He smiled at us, and his demeanour relaxed.

Pete was next to push the door open, ducking and removing his hat in one slick motion. He looked like an Italian businessman, immaculate right down to his waistcoat and wingtip boots. Pete had a knack for always maintaining a photogenic pose, so a photographer could have taken a snapshot and it would be magazine-ready, while a snapshot of me would have had me scratching my nose or taking a slurp of coffee.

A while later the door made a thumping sound before Cotton spilled through. He was energised to the point that he seemed more like a small crowd than a single person.

"Emery! How's the Man Upstairs? Pete, have you grown? Hahahah, I sound like your aunt. Harry! Looking good, man. Finn, you old dog, what are you up to?".

I wasn't sure if I was an 'old dog' by any description, but I was pleased to see everyone together again.

The Impressions were back in action.

CHAPTER SEVEN

No Room At the Inn

As I explained the events of the past twenty-four hours, it was interesting to watch the shift in demeanour of each person in the room. I could see the thoughts on their minds as they recalled that white-backed corpse in the water with its tangled hair and purple veins.

Cotton refused to sit down. He was pacing, flicking open the curtains every few minutes to stare out the window. Eventually, he paused for a moment, holding his head in his hands.

"I'm being followed," he said, "for the past year, I've had glimpses of someone that I know is tracking me. They've been in my home - I'm sure of it." The rest of us stared at him, and he changed tack. "Well, what if this is all related, I mean, like a wheel within a wheel. Two dead people, no suspects, and they both come back to me".

"Cotton, you didn't even know about this until today. I doubt some deranged stalker is going about hiding bodies in the hope that you'll stumble across them. That doesn't even make sense". I tried to be the voice of reason.

"It's quite possible, actually," Pete offered, "Cotton is famous, and peripherally related to a mysterious cold case. What if someone who knows about the Lady in the Lake is trying to set him up?".

"Then why not set all of us up, Pete?" Emery was concentrating, a forefinger against each temple. "Like the Pharaoh's Curse. We're all related to this, so we all stand to pose a threat, whether that's a physical one or a spiritual one".

Harry snorted. "I live in my parent's house - well it's mine, now, since they both died - and I do spreadsheets all day; ledgers, debits, credits. I wasn't even at the lake that day".

That much was true. I hadn't even known that his parents had died, but they'd never been socially active. His mother was obsessed with tidiness and didn't like us to visit. His father seemed like a shell of a man, withdrawn, who read his newspaper as if trying to hide from the world. Maybe they'd just pick it up off his armchair one day to find that he'd vanished, like those bizarre cases of people who'd spontaneously combusted, leaving nothing behind but a pair of smouldering slippers.

So far, their conspiracy theories hadn't offered an iota of insight, but I appreciated having them with me.

It was Cotton who initiated the reaction for what happened next.

"I'm booked in for the next few days until we sort this out. I can't go home; they'll *know*", he said, with a glance over his shoulder.

I looked over his shoulder. There was nothing to be seen. It worried me that his mental health had deteriorated to this point. Any further down that shady path, and he'd be a candidate for the asylum.

The others nodded.

"Ghosts, criminals or just bizarre circumstances - we're the team for the job," Pete said, standing up. "I get the feeling that we have to lay the past to bed, or, in this case, the grave." He gathered his overcoat over his sleeve with a wink. "Let me go and secure a room". He left.

"I'm just down the road", Harry ventured, "but I'll be around the next few days. Tax season is over, so I can afford to take a break". He laughed at what I assume was an accountant's joke he'd made to himself.

"Let the Impressions heed the call, then!" declared Emery, adding what I imagine he thought was a bold and fearless challenge to everyone in the room, like a Napoleonic general on horseback waving a cutlass at the moon.

Oh dear, I thought to myself. What have I done?

CHAPTER EIGHT

Harry's tale

There's a phenomenon that's well documented: when adult children who have moved away and lived adequately on their own terms spend time with their parents, it's not unusual for them to find themselves slipping into old patterns. That can affect how they speak (even using different accents) and how they act. It's not contrived, either, they just put on another character costume as if they were an actor in a play. I tended to do that when I saw my own parents from time to time, especially if my brothers were around.

My life had become like one of my own shelves, held neatly in place by the bookends of routine and contentment. While adults may daydream about the carefree memories of youth and lives free of responsibility, the reality is more stark. Kids in their teens are vulnerable in their *naïveté*, unaware of the perils that await. They'll need to go through an obstacle course of inevitabilities that will form the path to true adulthood, with grief, loss, disappointment and fear paving the way. A cynical way of viewing life, sure, but also not inaccurate.

Adults who lack the skills needed to succeed in life seem to skip the steps of coping with difficulty. It's especially easy to numb the thoughts with booze or drugs, but the truth is that should they ever get sober, the problems won't have disappeared, they'll still be there, queuing up for attention.

While I guessed that I had plenty of childhood issues to work through, my self-assessment was that I'd probably done a better job than Cotton, who seemed to be on the verge of a psychotic break. Emery had channelled his personality tweaks into his version of religion, while Harry had just rubber-stamped his own adulthood ticket as if it were an audited document. Pete had managed to retain both sides to his character: at once, sophisticated and in control and then, at the same time, quick to revert to the natural leader he'd been as a child, goading us into following him. It wasn't malicious or manipulative, it was just a natural dynamic that took over when we were together.

I thought back to when we were kids, and, for an instant, caught myself wondering if things could have turned out differently. For the longest time, I'd been hung up on Amelia Pickering. For most of two years, I just gawked at her in class, admiring the way she seemed comfortable in her own skin. She'd been among the first to graduate to socialising at the pubs, but she'd never given the impression that she was reliant on the loud, boorish young men who circled her like tiny sharks.

Once, when the band was becoming known in our town, I'd had my first grown-up conversation with her. She surprised me by being articulate and informed, and I blushed inwardly at my own ignorance. I realised that I'd just admired her appearance and her attitude and was horrified at how shallow I'd been. I was a bit taken aback that she hadn't warmed to Pete, first, with his air of sophistication, or to Cotton, a walking party animal who drew you into his endless energy like a human tornado.

For a time, we even had something of a relationship, but she was distracted; it was like meeting and dating someone at an airport, knowing they're heading off at any moment. Eventually, she did, choosing to work as an educational assistant to fund her Eurotrip, a trip that ended with her meeting a restaurant owner in Barcelona and settling there. The postcards eventually stopped coming, but there was never any ill will.

After that, I'd had a few romantic interludes, but I suppose there was a shadow behind my eyes after the incident of my childhood that never left. It made me intense but I wasn't great at speaking about my feelings, so anyone involved with me just sensed an emotional barrier. I wasn't lonely. I felt an irrational pride at being able to dwell alone with my own thoughts without going nuts.

As for the others, Harry had never married, Emery had a wife and two children, Pete travelled a lot and admitted vaguely that he may have had a son and Cotton had paternity suits. He'd had countless relationships, if the media was to be believed, some more serious than others and not restricted by gender. Given his mental state at the time I'd last known him, he probably couldn't tell you how many partners he'd had over the years, either. One reason or another, our crew hadn't been successful in maintaining long-term relationships, on average, although I wondered how balanced Emery's marriage was, or if it was one of those situations where the woman is expected to fulfil a quiet and subservient role while the man acts as high priest over the household.

When we were together, that began to make sense.

***

The following morning, we emerged from our rooms, meeting in the dark foyer below to have a weak coffee and a functional breakfast of cold meats, cereals and toast.

I led them outside and we walked up past my house. The bookshop was closed (since I wasn't there) but the door was open. Two cops stationed out front straightened up and watched as we strolled past, but we didn't speak to them.

My car was outside, so we got in and drove. Through the town, out into the fields, over the hills and into Lakeside. Cotton was wearing sunglasses, even though the day was overcast and he was subdued. Emery had called his family before we left, and Pete had somehow managed to maintain his appearance, wearing a dark blue suit with a matching hat. We stopped in front of Harry's house. I could see him glance out the window before switching off the lights and joining us.

"The most logical place to start..." said Pete, and we knew immediately that he meant the lake. It hadn't changed much, although the rowboats were padlocked to a length of chain that dipped into the mud in rusty, dirty arcs.

There was a *No Swimming* sign that listed to one side, with little pictures of what couldn't be done at the lake, including making fires, ball games, waterskiing and letting dogs off their leashes. None of those activities were on our agenda.

The lake was still a place of beauty. I remembered that some days, it was like a mirror, reflecting the blue skies and clouds, on others, it was a black void, as impenetrable to the eye as ink.

The patch of reeds where we'd seen her was gone, making it hard to imagine the scene as it had been so long ago, but as we watched, a huge white mute swan dropped out of the sky, skidding to a halt on the water with a clatter of wings, almost exactly where Shelley had been found. It felt like a sign. After swimming in a wide circle and dabbling its broad bill under the surface, it slapped its way back into the sky and drifted off over the trees.

"They used to eat 'em", said Cotton, "before they made it illegal. Imagine, Kentucky Fried Swan. The size of the box!". It was a stupid thing to say, the kind of banter we'd had as children, but none of us picked up on the riff.

"Lighten up, kids," he said, scuffing his boots into the mud. He was wearing a tracksuit with a hood, matching top and bottoms. A weird combination with the boots and sunglasses, but somehow, he carried it off. He began the painstaking process of rolling what I assumed was a joint, although it could just have been a cigarette, as I wondered how his body had managed to keep going.

I thought about the Shark, the monster trout that had been here so long ago. It was unlikely that it was alive, although bodies of water can contain curiosities, scientific anomalies like fish that turn out to live twice as long as previously thought or new species that had somehow evaded discovery, even in a place as mundane as a village lake.

Harry started to say something, then stopped. Drew in a breath and tried again.

"I think there's something I need to tell you all, but first, I need you to keep it quiet." He looked at Cotton, whose hooded head nodded, a puff of smoke drifting off towards the pier. Harry continued.

"I'm just an accountant, right, living alone in a small village. Only... I'm not. A few years back, a black car pulled up outside my house and two men got out. They came to my door and I guess they gave me an offer I couldn't refuse. I've been part of a small, anonymous wing of the government ever since. Mostly, I track international syndicates and money laundering, giving the right department the heads up when I come across shady deals. I don't do field work, but I do deal with some of the most dangerous criminal organisations in the country. From a distance, of course."

He stopped. Looked relieved, as if a massive weight had been lifted off his chest, then continued.

He went on at length about how he'd had to travel to different countries under an assumed name, attending meetings with people whose identities he couldn't be sure of, either. He'd got an additional computer to work on, running his own accounts on his primary computer and the investigative work on the other. He mentioned some high profile companies, too, brands recognisable from news stories and sponsorship deals of football teams. He said that he'd once been held up in a subway by masked men with guns, but they'd been scared off by a group of kids that had chosen that moment to do some graffiti tagging.

We gaped at him.

"Here's the deal; I can access all sorts of records through my work. Including criminal databases and details about crimes. Over the years, I've taken a closer look at anything that could be tied back to our Lady in the Lake. Back then, it was much harder to collate similar cases, especially across county lines and even country borders. You could have three bodies in almost identical circumstances but their geographical location would ensure that they weren't linked".

Pete was listening, hard. "So forget what *can't* be done, what *can* be done?", he asked.

Harry smiled. It wasn't a facial expression he used often, and it looked quite clumsy. "I've been reading up about anything to do with women who went missing in the 70s in this area and beyond. It's shocking. It really wasn't that long ago, but if you were vulnerable - a prostitute or drug addict - you could disappear and there'd hardly be a search for you. There was a 'no body, no crime' attitude, but even if there was a body and it couldn't be identified, the same rules would apply. There were quite a few women reported missing and only a couple ever turned up. One was an unidentified victim in a traffic accident, and one had drowned in the sea along the coast outside Shoreby, but they suspected she'd just walked into the waves during a bad time in her marriage."

"On the other hand", he continued, "there were plenty of archaeological digs around here over the years. The original inhabitants of these parts lived off the land and became part of it, so they're bound to surface from time to time. One particular site caught my eye, though. It made the news in history circles for yielding a hoard of ancient artefacts, including jewellery. You'll never guess what kind of jewellery, though...".

But we could.

He reached into his pocket and pulled out a few pieces of folded paper. They were pictures of archaeological dig records, marked with their location labels in fine, handwritten cursive writing. The writing identified what they were, but we knew without even reading.

Shell pendant. Shell broach. Shell hairpin.

Harry looked at us, as if trying to see what we were thinking. "You know, we can finally shut this thing down; I think we can. We need to".

It wasn't something I'd been prepared for. It brought back that summer when we'd become detectives. Bad ones, since we'd never made any headway. Inside, though, it felt like there was a young version of me who could see Shelley sitting up in the morgue in her white pinafore, scattering a handful of shells across the steel table and onto the tiles, her pale blue eyes without pupils gazing into the void. That vision had stuck with me for many years.

Pete had turned away from us to face back into the hills, but he spun around. "So we're thinking this is a student, a digger?" he said. "That's possible but she'd have been a documented part of a group".

Harry smiled again. "Not necessarily. I have a few ideas bouncing around, but I'd need you all to help out."

The problem was, I didn't know if I wanted to become that person again, connected to the news stories by bodies and violence. Cotton looked at his watch, trying to remember what day it was. "I've got a couple of days. Truth is, the album is on hold, so I can be here for a while. I need to get away from the madness, anyway."

I just wanted my house back, preferably without any bodies in the basement. It felt unfair. We could finally get rid of the one stigma of death, only for me to have to deal with another one. Alone.

"Let's go see about a shell necklace", Pete said, kicking a pebble across the beach and into the water at the edge of the lake.

CHAPTER NINE

The Seduction

We strolled back towards the car, trying to figure out a plan. We couldn't let on how we'd found the information about the shell artefacts, since Harry was adamant that he needed to be kept out of the paper trail. We needed to find out how to contact the archaeological team that had carried out the dig, if there were still any people around from those times. More than that, we needed the cold case file with the pictures of Shelley's body, especially her face, and the necklace itself.

We dropped Harry at home and headed back over the hill to Blacksea. At the inn, we went to our separate rooms. I left Pete leaning on the counter talking to the owner's daughter. She was giggling, and he was playing up to it, unbuttoning his shirt a bit and tilting his hat back like a 50s mobster.

A few minutes later, I heard him heading upstairs with her at his side. She was still laughing.

It amazed me that people could be so blasé about hooking up. Others seemed to just catch a glance, exchange a few words and then get right down to romance. I say romance, but it seemed to be strictly a physical act that was going on, with hearts stashed in the cupboard for safekeeping. I supposed they saw it as a natural thing, like going to the gym or for a jog, but together and horizontally.

There was still activity down at my house, which was a bit of a concern. They must have extracted the corpse by now, and I hoped they hadn't started excavating beyond that. At least the building was old enough to be protected so they couldn't just tear it down. If you were suspicious about bodies and bones in the soil, you'd have to tear down every city in the country, since they were all literally built on the backs of previous generations. The very soil underneath our feet was part leaves, part ancestors.

The phone rang. I picked it up, but no one was on the other end of the line, just a crackling noise for a few seconds and then a hard *click.* I went downstairs again but there was nobody at the front desk. There was, however, a burning smell coming from a door to the right of the entrance, so I knocked on it, pushed it open. The smell intensified and there was smoke, too. Covering my mouth with my jacket, I walked in and saw a large pot on the stove, boiling over. There were bits of meat on a chopping board and the coils of the stove were smoking and sizzling. I removed the pot and turned off the dial. A hand-written menu was on the table: rabbit stew, homemade, ice cream sundae. I guessed that the rabbit would be off the menu now, and that the woman upstairs with Pete had been tasked with keeping an eye on it.

The street was empty outside, so I headed to the police station to get some feedback.

The cop on duty nodded at me, flipped open the door to the back office and let me inside. The sergeant was facing the window, talking on the phone. She saw me arriving in the reflection and waved at me to sit. I sat. There was a beige folder open on her desk with pictures of my house, the storefront and what must have been the body. She slid another folder over the photos.

"Mr Jones. We're still in the preliminary stages of our investigation. I would like to ask you a couple of informal questions, though. Would that be alright?"

"Sure, go ahead".

"Have you ever kept a journal?"

"Not for years, no". If I had, I'd probably have kept that to myself.

"Why are your friends here?"

"We're all part of the club. That club we were members of by default, the one where you get to have a cloud over your head as a result of a murder. They know how it feels, and I wanted them with me while we sorted this new horror out".

"You do know that your friend, Cotton Ball, is part of an ongoing investigation into drug trafficking, right? And that Harald Berg is also the known associate of an international white collar crime syndicate?"

"Harry? Hell, no, I had no idea". I carefully avoided mentioning Cotton.

"There's more. Peter Fryer has been on the radar for years in relation to three separate assault cases. To round it off, Emery Bird is part of an organisation that has been described as a cult. Apparently, he holds a senior position in this organisation and it's just a matter of time before the hammer falls in numerous complaints against it".

There you go. My team of helpers had managed to get me under a cloak of suspicion that I'd probably never be able to shake off. I knew Cotton's lifestyle was chaos - everyone did - and Harry had admitted, somewhat shadily, to being privy to underworld activity. Emery's over the top religious connection was creepy but hadn't seemed criminal in any way.

As for Pete, I was devastated.

In films, the job of the screenwriter and director is to draw those lines: make sure that the hero really is the hero and the villain is easily identified. While novelists throughout time have enjoyed the concept of good vs evil, Cain and Able were two distinct people, while Jekyll and Hyde were cartoonish exaggerations of the id vs the superego. Pete had always been Abel, always Hyde. A gentle, wise and respected part of us. It went against his code, our code, to hurt other people.

"Sergeant, I'd not willingly hang out with the kinds of people you're describing. I may not have kept track of them over the years, but I think I'm a fair judge of character. I've lived in this village for over fifteen years and I've seen you around town. You've seen me, too. I'm not part of some twisted band of criminals and I've not personally committed a crime, either. What I *do* have is a body that was found in my basement and a shop that I can't open as a result."

"Mr Jones..."

"Please, call me Finn".

"Finn, Blacksea has never been the kind of town where we deal with hardcore crime. We just don't have these sorts of activities taking place. Bodies in bookshops, drugs, violence..."

"I get it, but I'm sure that body was there long before me. What my friends get up to when I'm not around and without my knowledge is none of my business, although I condemn criminal activity of any sort. I'm sure they'll get back to their lives, presently". I was getting defensive, and sounded like a teenager in trouble, even to myself.

"We have an idea about the origin of this body in your basement, but you'll need to give us some time to put it all together". She reached out and touched my hand involuntarily, realised what she'd done and whisked her hand away again.

"I'll stay where I am, then, and trust that you'll do what needs to be done. Please excuse me".

I got up, left the office and walked back outside. Heart thrumming. The sergeant was a conundrum: I liked her no-nonsense attitude, but not when I was the central point of her suspicions.

This brief conversation had left me complicit in a variety of issues that implicated each one of my friends, although, should any of the accusations prove to be true, it was more likely that they weren't friends at all. I was angry. The monstrous headlines waiting to be written were looming overhead. *"Drugs, Sex and Murder - Rock's Filthiest Band"*. The headline would have to be a lot longer to cover all the bases, but still, it was bound to appear in many, many iterations.

I felt it would be a terrible idea to confront them, each with their secrets, and that it was better to let the police do their investigations.

CHAPTER TEN

One Down

The minute I'd been asked to stay nearby, an ornery resistance kicked in. I wanted to be far away from this, the people and the situation. My passport was at home, though, probably still tucked into the small case I sometimes travelled with. Some people like to go on beach holidays, others aim for the sweaty nightclubs of party islands. I like to explore bookshops when I'm abroad, finding something homely and comforting about them. Even in different languages, you can feel welcomed in a bookish environment. I wouldn't be able to get on a plane right now, and I couldn't even enjoy my own bookshop. I headed to the library instead.

The library was an afterthought in Blacksea. A prefabricated building with the bare minimum. A long shelf of fiction, another for various categories of non-fiction and then a children's corner with a desultory collection of cushions and toys and some bedraggled picture books.

I got on well with the librarian, though. She was older than me, but she'd told me once that she thought of me as an "old soul", and that we both loved books because they were a haven from the world outside. That's probably because I had a tendency to lose track of conversations and stare into the distance with a manner that some would consider to be poignant and reflective, but I was more likely to be wondering how to turn the chicken pieces I'd taken out of the freezer into meals that would last two days.

Her name was Rosemary Coonan. She'd heard about my great aunt, but only because she'd been something of a legend in book circles in the area, able to find almost anything to fulfil requests, and locals had expected the librarian to have the same magic powers when she'd first started her job in the previous library building attached to the Town Hall. She was originally from up north, Yorkshire, and had a warm, welcoming burr to her voice.

"Rosemary! Great to see you. Reading anything interesting lately?"

"Ah, Finn. So sorry to hear about the… business… at your house. You know me, always with three books on the go at the same time; I wish I had an extra pair of eyes". She peered at me through a pair of spectacles so large they covered most of the top half of her face.

She carried on: "Then again, I'd need more time. Don't you think time is something we should recommend along with a book - time well spent, if you want my opinion".

"Of course, Rosemary. I spend most of my conversations now saying 'it feels like yesterday', because everything does. It's a trick!"

I asked if the library had any books available on local archaeology. She didn't think they had and dug out microfiche films to check catalogues. The library wasn't computerised just yet. I wandered up and down the shelves, neck at 45 degrees, checking the titles but not really looking for anything. A browse in a library is different to one in a bookshop. In a store, the books are usually only there for a short time before being sold. In a library, you could easily see the same book on the same shelf for years. I'd been coming here since I was a child, and most of the village had likely touched these same spines, too.

After a few minutes, she called me over.

"I've found a few titles you might be able to look for, but they're all academic, not something we'd have. I reckon you'll need to go to the Uni and ask them. There's an author who lives somewhere nearby, too. Lakeside, I think. Prof De Mink, a specialist in archaeology of some sort. I've seen him at the meetings." I think she was talking about Alcoholics Anonymous meetings but had forgotten that she wasn't supposed to reveal their names, but, I figured, her forgetfulness was my win. I wouldn't tell him who my source was. It's a small town, being part of the fellowship gave you limited anonymity, since everyone knew everything about everyone else.

Anyway: Lakeside. That felt like a bit of luck. I thanked her and she smiled as her head dipped back into the book she'd been reading.

Back over the hill. It was becoming a habit.

There were sheep dotted among the fields, fenced in on three sides with the river on the fourth so they couldn't wander onto the narrow roads fringed with cow parsley and nettles that separated Blacksea from Lakeside. When I was young, a full stand of old oaks had marked the border of the village, but most of them had toppled in different storms, and there were just two left. The remains of the other trees had been carted away and used as firewood, probably, but that left space for a meadow that produced a rainbow of colour at the right time of year; wildflowers and weeds. A low stone wall with an ancient stile in place brought you into the village itself if you'd been rambling up on the hills.

I went to the house where my parents had lived - where I'd lived - and looked up at what used to be my bedroom window. My parents had moved south to the coast, into a single storey cottage in a retirement complex. I saw them occasionally, but we mostly just carried on with life without bothering each other.

Glancing around the village, I realised I could close my eyes and map it from end to end with almost perfect accuracy.

The small church with its slate roof and yellow stone walls. The yew trees in the graveyard that may once have yielded branches for longbows. A new garage door on the Hopkin's property at the bottom of the hill, replacing the one that had been damaged in an accident when a visitor misjudged the grade of the road and the turn at the bottom. It was familiar. There was a house with a front garden that was almost entirely a hutch filled with chickens and ducks. The hutch contained a small pond.

If you'd connected my former house with those of my friends with lines on a map, you'd almost have a pentagon that covered the perimeter of the village. I liked the expression 'as the crow flies'; as a child, I'd tried to imagine the village from above in the few seconds it would have taken a crow to drift across.

Up to the north, Pete's place. A semi-detached cottage with a new roof that had replaced the original dull thatch. Almost opposite, Emery's double-storey house, an impressive size compared with the other properties next to it. There was Cotton's former house. An insignificant place, but it sometimes had bunches of flowers dumped next to the front door by fans, making it appear to be a makeshift memorial. The current owners didn't mind, they just left the flowers and soft toys outside. Harry's house was the kind of shape you'd expect to see if you asked a child to draw a house. One tree in the front garden. A straight path that led through an immaculate lawn to an ordinary place with rose bushes in front of the windows and a chimney, top left.

I popped in at the newsagents on the corner of Lake Road to ask if they knew where Professor De Mink lived, and the owner came outside to point it out. It was the old Pickering place.

He was pretty ancient, the professor, but he became animated when he realised I was looking for any brochures, booklets and books on his favourite topic. I got the impression that he'd overused that topic of conversation with everyone else in town and wasn't able to chat much about it anymore.

He described that it had been like back then, with students

descending on every dig to have extended parties. Some stayed in caravans and tents to keep their costs low, and the rumours about what went on were colourful, the villagers using low tones to whisper about scandalous behaviour. He started to tell me some of the more lascivious tales before seeing my face and realising that I wasn't that invested in hearing about students having sex twenty years ago in a field.

"I'll get it all back to you," I said, as he waved me off.

"Not to worry, lad, it's more use to you than it is to me".

He'd given me a large box of booklets and documents he thought I'd like to check out. It was heavy, so I dumped it in the boot of the car. I left him with his daydreams of muddy parties long gone.

It was time to go and see how the others were getting on, so I drove back into Blacksea, parked outside the inn. Pete was standing outside, smoking. I'd forgotten that he did that. The cigarette looked like a prop in the hands of a Golden Age of Cinema actor.

"Bit of a morning," he offered. I nodded. Emery was inside with Cotton. They were deep in conversation and took a moment to look up when I entered the room. Cotton looked awful. He was scratching at his neck, leaving big, red welts and his eyes were watering. Emery looked neat, as if he'd dressed for a sermon flyer picture. He was wearing a grey striped tie that made him look like a salesman, but I suppose he was, in a sense.

"What's up?" I asked. Pete was standing behind me. I filled them in on some of the details, mostly the ones to do with the information about the digs and the box of literature I'd retrieved.

It took a few minutes before we remembered that Harry wasn't in the room. Maybe that's why he'd been recruited as an agent of some sort: he just blended in (or out) with ease. You could spend an afternoon with him and forget he was there, making us useless as any kind of alibi. The hotel phone rang.

Thirty seconds later, the young woman I'd seen with Pete put her head around the door.

"It's the police," she said. She was shaking a bit. "Your

colleague, Mr Berg has been found. He had a note on him with your names and the name of the inn on it. They described him to me and I'm sure it's your… friend". She wasn't sure whether we worked with him or he was just a mate, but she was certain it was him from the description the police had given. "He, he, I'm-so-sorry, he's dead".

Harry. Dead. What? I was thinking in single syllables. That's not true, I was just round there this morning. I immediately panicked at that thought: *"Bookshop Suspect Seen in Deadly Coincidence"*, the headlines would read. My head was all over the place, to the point that I thought that if we ever got back together as a band, we'd have to be acoustic if we had no drummer. The first of the Impressions to go. Unthinkable.

Cotton was losing it. I don't know if it was the drugs, the withdrawals or just his general mental state, but he was vibrating with a terrifying energy. "No, no, no, no," he repeated. "No-no-no-no-no-no". He ripped off his leather jacket and slumped into an armchair, sweating. Emery's eyes were closed. At first, I thought he was praying, but then he surprised all of us by swearing, loudly and then bursting into tears.

Pete turned on his heels and went back outside, sliding a packet of cigarettes out of his pocket as he left and swinging one between his lips in one swift move.

The inn was about to become yet another point in some convoluted investigation. I imagined that the police had a murder wall with red threads connecting different elements: our black and white photos, old news articles. Crime scene pictures and a few theories about how it was all connected.

They didn't need a murder wall, I was starting to think that it really was all connected, as disparate and bizarre as each new part of the story became. If they didn't have a murder wall, I'd want to help them start one myself, but they'd probably not let me, since I was not only a civilian, but a suspect of an as-yet-to-be-defined crime.

CHAPTER ELEVEN

Column Inches

We waited at the Inn for the police; we knew they'd turn up, and they did, just two of them, Sergeant Stanbury and her colleague. They were grim-faced, not as easy going as they had been previously. She looked at each one of us in turn, as if assessing if she could take us on in a fight.

"It'll be easier to chat to you here rather than get you all down to the station at the moment, so let's keep this informal".

"What happened, Sergeant?" Pete was the first of us to speak.

"We can't disclose much, but what we can tell you is that your friend, Harald Berg was found deceased this morning by a Lakeside police officer. The circumstances give us reason to believe that his death was neither a natural one nor an accident".

She left that hanging in the air as we filled in the blank.

"So he was killed by someone?", I asked. "That's just nonsensical. He's an accountant, for goodness sakes. I can't imagine he had valuables around the house, either".

Stanbury pivoted towards me, rolling in her wheeled office chair that someone had brought into the room.

"That's just it, Finn, we believe he wasn't just your regular accountant. We suspect he was the middleman for a number of serious crimes".

She's already said as much to me, so she was saying this for the benefit of everyone else, I surmised, but it still felt like there was a gap in their intelligence. Harry had intimated that he'd been recruited as an undercover informant of some sort, but we couldn't tell the police that, whoever Harry had been working for would need to put the brakes on their investigation into his death.

Stanbury smiled at me, but it was the smile of a person who's holding the winning cards. "We know you were all close, and we're aware of your association with the Lakeside cold case from the 70s. If any of you have any details that can help us to put Harry to rest, I suggest you let us know sooner rather than later".

She paused, leaving a gap of silence that we knew we were supposed to fill, whether with protestations of innocence or indignation, but we knew that any kind of response would add fuel to their suspicions. We looked at each other like naughty kids in the principal's office.

"We've not been close with Harry for many years," Emery said, finally, "That poor man had isolated himself from us and most other people. As for the cold case: that went cold almost twenty years ago, and we've barely thought about it since. I'd like the chance to discuss with my friends an appropriate send off for Harry; I guess we were his closest friends, no matter how far away we were in life."

Emery sounded a bit like a pastor pitching for the chance to conduct a wedding (or, in this case, a funeral), but, since Cotton, Pete and I were somewhat allergic to religion, he was probably the best person for the job.

Pete concurred. "It's a tragedy, no doubt. And yes, we have life-long ties to this area and to Harry, of course. We'd very much like to be kept informed about this investigation".

"Whatever you need", Cotton added. We can make a

contribution to whatever fund supports the local coppers".

Stanbury's eyes narrowed. "We have public funding, Mr Ball. I suggest you keep your money in case you need it for an emergency. You never know when you need a *stash*". She emphasised that last word with contempt.

Cotton reddened. He looked out the window, didn't reply.

I followed his gaze. A car I hadn't seen before was outside the door of the inn. It was one of the newer Volvos and looked expensive. A man was leaning against it, holding a notebook and surveying the place. He looked like he was from the city, given his suit and tie. Apart from Pete, suits and ties weren't the local dress code.

Stanbury and her colleague excused themselves, with a directive for us to get in touch. The man outside made a note in his book, got into his car and followed them at a slight distance.

His name turned out to be Ellis Crocker. I didn't need to be a detective to find out that he was the journalist responsible for the headlines I saw, real ones this time: "Tragic Twist In Lake Cold Case" and "Famous Drummer Dies As Mystery Corpse Appears". The newspapers seemed to revel in this cocktail of murder, fame and mystery.

The mad idea that our short-lived band from the late 70s could be linked to this mess was further proof that no one could figure any of it out. Despite myself, I smiled at the way Harry had been termed a famous drummer, since the very concept of fame is what drove him back to the village to live in relative seclusion.

Worse still, the press in general had picked up on a story with potential and, inevitably, they'd dug up our music. As we gathered around the TV, we were shocked to hear the opening bars of Lady in the Lake:

"She's a lady, make no mistake,
Where others bend she had to break,
In the reeds upon the lake.
Do you hear the wind in the trees,
Look there and you might see me,
Can you see she's swimming free,

The lady, the lady in the lake".

I cringed. I think we'd all written those lyrics, each one of us contributing a line, which gave it a nonsensical, juvenile feel. But we'd been nonsensical and juvenile ourselves, at the time. Once again, I thought about those pop stars who are locked into singing trivial tunes and lines decades later. The ones who made a fortune of it and the ones who were still trying to stay above water financially. I was immediately glad I'd not been woven into that cycle of despair.

Cotton was in a more precarious position, since his subsequent fame had dwarfed any contribution the Impressions he'd made in his early career. He risked losing a lot of credibility.

The laaaady of the laaaake. Ah, it was a terrible earworm, but it was effective: once you'd got it stuck in your mind, it was like glitter, you'd never get rid of it. From experience, though, I knew the media would tire of it quite quickly: journalists would use the case as an excuse to spend a few days in the countryside before being recalled to the never-ending news cycle in the city, where murders, violence, drugs and political intrigue were the order of the day.

CHAPTER TWELVE

Lake Kids Get Relief

Harry's death turned out to be a turning point in this whole mess.

Emery became the hero of the moment, putting together a funeral that was at once bizarre and fitting, a combination of his cult-adjacent background and the rock 'n roll spin he opted to put on Harry's death. The media joined *en masse*, filming us as we trudged around in black clothes and sunglasses around the village, as if we were filming some morbid rock video instead of mourning a friend.

Better yet, it turned out that the coroner was in one of his home cells, so he was able to find out more details about Harry's death than we'd otherwise have known.

Strangled and sliced open like a fish from chin to groin. His screams had been heard for a short time early in the morning that he'd been found. A neighbour had called the police, who discovered Harry's door open, and his body slumped over piles of papers on his desk, hands tied into the cord around his neck as if he'd tried to claw it off.

One detail sent chills down our spines: in his throat, three shells had been wedged, with two more in his stomach.

His home computer had been destroyed. Not just wiped, but completely obliterated. We assumed that the other computer had been taken, since we could only see the remains of one PC. A paper note was found that may or may not have been important, listing our names and the name of the Primrose Inn. The cryptic words "NOT AGAIN" had been scrawled on the note - by Harry, or someone else - it wasn't clear.

Pete had been hard at work in the local pub, charming journalists and making them laugh at his stories. He'd won them over, but he'd been calculating in this, knowing that the national attention may trigger closer investigation of what had happened both then and now.

As predicted, the local cops became less animated about finding the root of Harry's murder. Presumably, the word had come down that they needed to back off. Some black-suited heavies arrived one morning and cleared out Harry's entire house, every last bit of furniture, into a moving van. They drove away, leaving a piece of police tape flapping in the autumn wind at his front door.

Emery moved back home with his wife and kids, although he, too, managed a friendly wave at any journalists who hung about.

Cotton seemed to take it hardest of all. He'd had a full career in an industry loaded with unnatural dangers and had lost bandmates, lovers, fans and friends to drugs and mental health-related issues over the years. As a young man, he'd survived the heady excesses of the 80s, but not without engaging in some of his own. A charismatic singer, he'd been able to keep the band in the charts by sticking to the patterns of popularity. As keyboard-driven tunes lost their following, he added more guitar. Then, when guitar got out of hand with the hair bands, he made sure to adapt by bringing out some surprisingly tender acoustic songs, bordering on folk. He wasn't part of the most recent shifts in musical tastes, but he had enough of a following and street cred to maintain ticket and album sales. He'd also collaborated with the right people at the right time, so what he lacked in his own creative style, he gained from theirs.

There had been a news story about him waking up in bed with a woman who had overdosed, but his role in that was peripheral: she was a known addict who'd been around anyone in the industry with money and drugs to offer, and the pills she'd taken weren't linked to Cotton in any way, they were from a ten-year-old stash she'd remembered that she'd hidden in the roof tiles of a clinic, so she faked a period of recovery to get them back. (She'd been indiscreet and told everyone around her big plan, too). Those pills weren't even in circulation anymore - and, after she swallowed a handful of them - neither was she.

The strange thing about addiction is that it doesn't affect everyone the same way. Some don't burn out, they light up and stay smouldering. Others peak with jaw-dropping speed, going from living as teetotallers to rock bottom in the space of a few months. From what he'd said to me on the few occasions we had caught up over the phone, he seemed to live a cyclical life of ups and downs, getting high, getting clean, going on tour, staying at home; managing to avoid joining the 27 Club and the tragic obituary pages in the music mags.

Of all of us, he was closest to Pete, giving Pete the okay to perform in session recordings with friends in the industry. Pete was happy to turn up with his gear, come up with some bass riffs that formed the backbone to some well-known hits, and then retreat to his life in the betting shop. He had gained a reputation of his own as a respected musician, but then bass players tend to gain and crave adulation less than lead guitarists or vocalists. He went on summer tours around Europe, filling in where regular musicians had fallen out with the band or had been too ill to travel. He sent me pictures when he was on the road, I guess so I could live the life of a rock star vicariously.

Cotton and Pete stayed at the Inn. Cotton's winter tour wasn't in rehearsal yet and Pete seemed to like the sabbatical he'd been taking from life. They spent a lot of time at the pub, almost becoming locals, blending in with the farmers, pensioners and groups of youngsters.

As for me, after a few days, I was allowed to return to my home and the bookshop.

The sergeant had come to visit me at the Inn to let me know, and she'd come with me as I carried my bags back into the house from the car. She'd said that it was so that I could check that nothing was missing, but I suppose she was going above and beyond her mandate.

I offered her coffee, but we ended up in bed.

It could have been the weeks of tension, the fear, the emotions at losing a friend and the sheer feelings of being overwhelmed, but I saw her differently. As if the moment she crossed over the threshold into the house, she became achingly beautiful. I knew, then, what it must be like for Pete, to recognise a spark in each other's eyes. A longing that came from nowhere and spilled over.

She'd looked at me, started to say something and then stopped. Maybe putting her inner voice out of earshot. I'd been distracted with my bags, but as I turned around, she was close to me, the hairs on my arms stood up. We just moved closer until we were clasped in each other's arms, eyes closed, lost in the moment. We bumped our way upstairs to the bedroom, trying to remove our clothes at the same time, not caring about the clumsiness of it all. She was strong and expressive, guiding my hands and holding my back.

Afterwards, she seemed quite different from the cop I'd known at the station. She was gentle, whispering, a little out of breath. I'd traced my finger down her spine and over her hips, while she touched my neck, cupping the back of my head in her hand and ducking down toward my chest, her dark hair shining in the lamplight.

Although I'm usually an awkward person to be around, I managed to avoid making any jokes to interrupt this moment of intimacy. I figured that, being a policewoman, she'd likely encountered too many clumsy pick-up lines about being under arrest from desperate men in bars.

We did manage to have coffee, tidy ourselves up a bit. I think I was blushing, but that's not such a bad thing to see in another person.

As she left, she made sure to let me know that I'd get a report on the body in the basement, so that reset the encounter and made it professional again, but she did it with her head tilted to one side in a way that felt right.

Leila. First, she'd been Sergeant. Then Sergeant Stanbury. Finally, Leila. I liked the way she called me Finn, too. The way she said it with a smile.

Home.

I wasn't ready to welcome customers into the shop, I wanted the cellar story to die down so I could open up the doors without having to tell and retell the story. The good thing about owning your own business is also the bad thing: you can take a break when you want to, but you also need to stay open when you don't want to. Right now, though, I had enough in my savings to cover the shortfall.

Besides, the shop was in a state of disarray. I could tell that the teams of people who'd been in and out had attempted to tidy up, but the intrusion was still visible. There were plastic sheets folded up and placed in corners, piles of books that had been cleared to make a wider path through the store and rubbish bags with fast food wrappers and paper coffee cups. I called Lucien, and he was there almost before I hung the phone, almost smiling under the tilt of his beret.

It took the rest of the day to put things in order, to dust off the cardboard display boxes that'd be reused, stack up some new titles and to change the window display. To my horror, I'd realised that the entire time that forensic teams had been coming and going, the window had been filled with a bold set of crime novels and posters. The posters offered blood-splashed teasers of the books they promoted, and I'd even added a little plastic coffin that had come with one of the marketing kits. Great job, I thought to myself. We replaced them with some travel and gardening books. Anything I could find that looked less bloodthirsty.

At the end of the day, I strolled back to the Inn, settled my bill and met with Cotton and Pete. They looked a bit worse for wear, since they'd been drinking for the past week as if in training for a booze-themed sport event.

"I had a call," Pete said. "The label execs wanted to reissue our album. Apparently, Lady in the Lake has been featured as the soundtrack to a TV series and there's a lot of interest in the retro sound".

I tried to imagine what kind of awful show would be able to work that song into its theme but failed. "Sure, I mean, it's been years since the last vinyl pressing, I'm certain being on CD would help", I offered. You couldn't really control the demand for these things - the music industry was mad like that - what you thought would sell, didn't and what you speculated was dead gained new legs from time to time. It was funny to have our music described as 'retro'.

An idea occurred to me. "What if we used the album to get to the bottom of the real cold case? We could add a booklet with all the details and even some pictures. Some fans are obsessive enough to follow up, and maybe someone has the resources to do something about it".

"That's a damned fine idea". Cotton had sat up straight. "You know, it's been twenty years. Surely crime busting has become more *sciency*."

Pete nodded. "DNA. They can do all sorts with that nowadays. I read that they'd caught a man and found him guilty of murder after fifteen years because of DNA he'd left on the body. You know: semen or spit, I guess."

I barely even cared about who had killed her, I just wanted to find out who she was, and DNA seemed like a reasonable place to start.

"I think those tests are specialised and expensive, so if we reissue the album, we could fund the tests. Maybe do it in honour of Harry."

They nodded.

"I'll make some calls", Pete said, and Cotton agreed, too. Between the two of them, they'd be able to leverage the influence to get this done.

Shelley, you've got a chance, I thought.

CHAPTER THIRTEEN

Why have you forsaken me?

I took a drive. A winding, aimless drive. Without thinking about it, I ended up at a place I hadn't been to in years, an old chapel that was set in the middle of farmlands rather than in a village. It was a place where ramblers stopped to sit in the shade for a while; as far as I knew, it wasn't used as a weekly place of worship.

The cemetery had a few graves that had been pushed askew by tree roots, with one stone angel having fallen onto her back among the dandelions. It was a place of peace, where I daydreamed of centuries past, of people walking here across muddy paths to nod their respects at the dead, a place where badgers and foxes ducked through the shadows at night.

Religion like that I could understand, a religion not tainted by greed nor ceremony, just a mood that came out of the soil, connecting people to their history. Again, I thought of Shelly, wondering if she'd ever walked these hills, if she'd stopped to taste the blackberries or to smell the scent of the lilacs and meadowsweet that attracted lazy bees and other insects. Maybe she'd been a person more attracted to the ocean that crashed onto the coast to the south, taking delight in squeezing foam-dampened sand between her toes.

It gave me pleasure to think of her alive, at one with nature, instead of recorded frozen in black and white pictures in a cold case file. Those images were not her.

I spent the afternoon watching the clouds barrel overhead, rolling in on themselves like waves and bursting up into the atmosphere with the promise of thunder.

I got back home in the early evening, there were more cars than usual on the main road. As I opened my front door, the phone rang. My relaxed moment was gone.

"Finn. Bad news". It was Pete. "It's Emery".

The cycle just never seemed to end. As one event appeared to be reaching closure, another would shift into focus.

It turned out that Emery was dead, too. Talk around town mentioned a possible gas leak, but that didn't make sense. He was a cautious person, more so than the rest of us. I remembered him saving my life, once, by checking that our equipment was safe at an outdoor festival when a rain shower drifted over. He uncovered some sparking wires and refused to play unless they were fixed, which they were. My guitar still felt alive with electricity, though, and my hair stood on end throughout the concert.

That was Emery: he saw the potential for disaster where the rest of us just carried on. Maybe that was what had set him on his religious path, always looking for ways to avoid becoming a victim.

It wasn't like Harry, whose death was clearly suspicious, so we found out more about what had happened.

Emery hadn't turned up at work. His assistant had gone round to the house and found the entire family laid out in a row in the lounge, completely dressed as if posing for a family picture. The place stank like gas, so the assistant had turned off the stove and called for medical assistance.

He'd said that their faces were blue, but apart from that, they seemed undisturbed, almost as if they were taking a nap on the floor. The staged attempt at murder-suicide failed, however. The paramedics were able to coax the children and Emery's wife back to life, although they were in a critical state when admitted. Emery wasn't that lucky, though.

She'd become Sergeant Stanbury again. At my door, looking serious.

"It's getting out of control", she said, "I think it could be my fault". At that, she smacked the door open and started crying at the same time.

"How could it be your fault? Did you turn on the gas?" I wasn't sure what else to say.

"I'd given him a call to ask him to come down to the station, and, well, shit, I let on that he and his organisation were under investigation. Next thing I know, the whole family's put at risk!".

Emery had never explained himself to me. I felt like there were a few red flags in his behaviour, in the same way that if you saw a street preacher, you'd cross the road to avoid being called out by them. The fact that his wife and kids seemed to stay indoors all the time didn't give any clues about what might have been going on. The group kept to themselves, too, not proselytising in the neighbourhood. She'd mentioned a cult, but I didn't know much about cults, except that I'd imagined them to be people wearing robes with long hair. Emery always looked like he was just another office worker with bad taste in grey suits and ties.

How did he go from being a regular person in a rock band to heading up a cult? And what horrors had he committed that he'd felt the need to take himself and his family off the board?

Once again, I thought of Cotton and his wild life, and how if anyone, he'd have been the most likely to die young, not Harry or Emery. Cotton had his own band of followers but that was a different scenario, he wasn't trying to brainwash them.

If anything, I'd brought them all to town, placing them

together at the same time for the first time in years. I couldn't fathom what forces were at work but felt sure that I was more responsible than anyone else for their deaths, whether by murder or suicide.

"Leila, you can't tell what goes through people's minds, especially if they're in a cult. The whole point of being in a cult is that you want to think differently, you accept being taught a different way of thinking. No one can predict the outcome of that".

"Yeah, but I let on that we had him in our sights. That's not professional. I'll probably lose my job over this, but it's still worse for his family".

Just then, a memory popped into my head. I wasn't even inventing it to make her feel better.

"I just had a flashback. Emery once said to me that he'd fixed his own brain. After the thing with the Lady in the Lake, he'd found a way to control his feelings. He said that he suddenly understood that we're just here temporarily and that death wasn't a sad thing, it was less painful than stubbing your toe. He had zero fear about it. Of course his family didn't deserve to be dragged into his delusions, but his lack of humanity wasn't your fault. It made sense to him."

Leila wasn't convinced.

Several cars had driven past us over the past few minutes. They looked like they were going on holiday, full to the roof with bags and clothes. At least three of them had stickers on the back with the name of Emery's organisation on them, and I realised these people were getting out of town before the investigation heated up. Whatever Kool Aid their low-rent version of Jim Jones had taken, they weren't going down with that ship. Emery's Jim Jones impression had been a sad, final whimper.

Another thing occurred to me. "You probably shouldn't be talking to me, either. Aren't I still a suspect in the basement body case?"

She winced. "Seeing as I'm screwed now, I may as well let you know. That body was taken in its entirety to the university. It's being kept in the morgue area where they store the cadavers for medical students. It's early days, but you need to know, you're off the hook, unless you're over 700 years old".

I stared at her.

"It's a peat body. Just a relic from the past that somehow managed to emerge under your house, in your basement. All we know is that she appears to be centuries old, and that her body was preserved by bog acids, a lot like vinegar. She was pickled long before this village even existed. I couldn't tell you until the official report came out, and, of course, the academics are all bickering about who gets to release their study first, but it wasn't a contemporary murder, even if she was bumped off back in the day. I'm so sorry."

What do you say to that? I felt like I'd dragged my old friends into something that wasn't to do with us at all. Even though it wasn't my fault, two of them were dead.

"What is strange, though," Leila continued, "is that we're pretty far away from the seaside, and under this woman's body was a midden of shells and bones, so there was an initial connection we had to check out. She had an ankle bracelet with shells on, too, but that was as common then as someone having pierced ears nowadays."

I laughed. Despite myself. I wasn't doing a great job of displaying appropriate emotions at the moment, but this was a relief.

This news changed my position on the spot. Once again, I was just a regular village bookseller, even if I was one who'd played in a band a long time ago and I'd once found the body of a woman in a lake. The fact that both bodies had been wearing shells was a curiosity, not a clue.

I had no particular reason to be loyal to Emery, either. "It's not your fault, Leila, none of this".

She took my face in her hands, "Don't you think you should just walk away from all this? You don't owe those guys anything,

especially not for some twenty-year-old cold case. I'm worried about you, there're just too many complications. Your friends seem to attract trouble, and while I understand Harry didn't deserve to die, the fact that we don't know who killed him is terrifying. Can't you drop it for a while until we can get more information and keep you safe in the meantime?"
It wasn't a bad idea, but all these cases had a hold on me. It wasn't that I wouldn't let them go, for some reason, I *couldn't*. She saw my expression of defeat,
She headed back to the police station, looking drained.

CHAPTER FOURTEEN

Home again, home

At the inn, the mood was sombre.

Cotton and Pete were both angry, feeling betrayed. Our feeble attempt at helping solve the cold case by releasing an album that no one would want to listen to in a few months felt inadequate. Harry, murdered. Emery's family horror. It was more than we could cope with.

Between the two of them, they'd decided to get back to whatever lives they could. Cotton was due to tour Europe, mainly just clubs, since he was trying to avoid the security risk that came with a big stadium. He said he'd try and push the Impressions re-release, but that he really wanted to just move on. He also claimed that he'd be spending a few weeks in rehab after the winter tour was over, saying that he wasn't as young as he used to be. None of us were.

Pete was subdued, but he tried to cover that up. "Chin up, guys, we're not done yet. We may just be three musketeers left, but it's up to us to hold the flag high". I wasn't even sure what that meant. He'd been drinking. The booze-soaked bravado that people use to get themselves through the day.

"I'll let you know if there's any news," I said, but the news at the moment was full of Bosnian atrocities and the O.J. Simpson trial. Our tiny story had started to slip to the middle pages.

We said our goodbyes.

I opened up the bookshop again, with customers gradually starting to return. At first, I got some stares, but then things settled down.

I was seeing Leila, off and on. She'd had a disciplinary hearing but then they'd found in her favour, especially since no one could have predicted such a calamitous outcome to what had been a careless slip in her professional behaviour. In fact, after a couple of months, she became DI Stanbury, which I reckoned she deserved. We were comfortable with each other, neither one looking to put the other under pressure with talk of a commitment.

She had a surprisingly wicked sense of humour, and I was glad to have someone to talk to rather than the voices in my head. She'd decided to stay in town rather than take up a more important role in the city, and I was just glad to go for long walks with her, drive down to the sea, or eat candy floss at a local fete, with fireworks blasting overhead. Her face lit up at simple pleasures, and that's all either one of us wanted: contentment.

To complete the settling down of chaos, TS the cat returned, acting as if she'd never been away, just easing down in front of the fire one evening.

The Impressions album got its re-release on CD. The album ticked over with some sales, but then a major band did a cover of Lady in the Lake, a far better version than we'd done originally, and it went to Number 1 in the charts. I'd made my peace with hearing it over shop PAs and on the car radio. It still reminded me of being kids, skidding through puddles on our bicycles, blissfully unaware of the ways life would send us spinning to the curb.

A year or so passed by after I'd found the body in the basement. I'd checked in with the university and they gave me the go ahead to carry on sorting out the cellar the way I'd planned on doing it. My original ideas had changed, somewhat. I felt like it was appropriate to honour this woman who'd rested beneath the house for so long in her comfortable bed of peat. In the corner where I'd found her, I set up a small fireplace, connecting the flue to the bigger fireplace above. This felt like a celebration of the elements of which she'd been a part.

Cotton seemed to have followed through with his plans of getting clean and had even been on TV talking about his new-found sobriety. He fobbed off any questions about Emery or Harry and the cold case, though, stating that he "lives in the present, that's all that counts". Perhaps he'd finally started listening to the advice of his publicity team. I'd asked Leila about his drug cases, but she refused to tell me anything. It soured the atmosphere between us if I did that, so I left it alone. He'd also released a biography of sorts, although it must have been ghostwritten, since it mangled the facts and I couldn't believe that he'd have forgotten so much, even if he had an entire poppy field or a mountain of snow in his veins. I was dismissed as the book guy, the one who had missed out on a world of fame by choosing to run a bookshop, and I suppose that was true. It was a relief, actually, to become a disposable bit part in his melodrama.

Occasionally, a big story would hit the news about organised crime and money laundering and I'd wonder if Harry's undercover role had anything to do with the busts. I hoped so, since it would feel unfair if he'd died for nothing.

Emery's cult had turned out to be a tiny one, and it died with him. His family vanished. He wasn't buried in Lakeside. I had no idea where they'd taken his body and didn't care, either.

Pete had almost disappeared. I'd get an envelope with photos in it every few months. He'd decided to travel the world as he had when he was younger, and, by the looks of things, was managing to do that at quite a rate. He also appeared to be making friends wherever he went, with doe-eyed girls wrapped around him on beaches and at swimming pools, waving their caps at the camera with palm trees in the background. He'd be grinning behind mirrored sunglasses, the light reflecting off a stubble that appeared to be going silver.

I'd not forgotten about those assault cases and had made a few enquiries of my own, without telling Leila. It seems like he'd been an enforcer for the betting shop, doing more than just taking the odds. He even had a specific routine that set him apart and got him flagged as a person of interest in several similar cases. There were rumours that he had a grid of tattoos across his shoulder where he'd commemorate a successful beating with an X, but that could just have been speculation. If you had defaulted on paying the bookies, you'd probably be living in fear of encountering a man of Pete's height with tattoos like that.

He was so charming that if he knocked on your door, you'd invite him in, too, before realising your mistake.

There were some cases open, but he'd not been arrested or charged, so he was able to travel under his own name. I'd accepted that I'd known far less about my former bandmates than I thought I had, and also that each of us got to choose which paths we followed in life. He looked calm in his photos, so I suspected he'd left that life behind, anyway, choosing to drift around islands and coasts, maybe playing at karaoke bars for kicks every now and then.

I got a parcel one Tuesday morning that fired up the old mixer again, sending all the ingredients of the past spinning together, mangled and indistinguishable.

CHAPTER FIFTEEN

Reverse whirlpool

It was one of those stuffed, yellow envelopes. Padded. In it, a note marked "From a friend. Xxx". The kisses made it feel creepy, but that was nothing compared with the rest of the contents. There was another envelope, the kind you'd get from an old photo development booth at the store, filled with pictures. The pictures were of me,, Harry, Emery, Cotton and Pete, as teens. The faded pictures looked exactly how you'd expect photos from the 70s to look: too much red and orange, not enough blue. A typed note said, in lowercase letters. "remember the past its still here" without any punctuation. I didn't want to remember the past at all, but this person clearly did.

As I slid everything back into the padded envelope, I noticed a tiny slit in the bubblewrap. Inside, yet another tiny envelope. This one held a piece of paper with a signature on it and a single, smooth shell. *Harald M. Berg.*

There we were, stuck in the past once again.

Leila wasn't happy. She'd hoped that the events of the previous year had ironed themselves out, and it frustrated her that I couldn't seem to drop the cold case. I insisted to her that it wasn't me that was digging things up, but that I was just a part of it by default.

The shell was what got to both of us. It was more than just a collection of photos and cryptic notes, this was a message, but the message was lost in time or, at least, it was missing enough parts for it to lose its meaning.

I took a drive with her over to Lakeside. I'd not done that before. I walked her through the village, showed her where we'd all lived and just how close everything was. We strolled down to the lake, where a flock of ducks was squabbling over some bread that a young mother and a child had just tossed off the pier. They were watching as the birds riled up the water, hand in hand. Leila shivered, although it wasn't cold, as if she'd remembered something she'd read in the cold case file.

"It was spring, right?" she asked.

"Yeah, well, almost summer. We weren't afraid of falling in the water that day, so it must have been warm enough".

"What's strange, then, is that the body was so intact. The insects had barely moved in, and this lake is right next to the nature reserve over the hill. There are plenty of carrion birds like crows that would have picked up the scent right away."

I looked up. As if summoned, two black shapes wheeled into view, crows looking to get in on whatever action the ducks were enjoying.

"I mean, you were kids, so you wouldn't have known all the details, but even her eyes were intact, they'd just faded a bit from the water".

She wasn't wrong. Shelley's back was smooth and white, like marble, fringed on the edges with purple. I'd not seen her face in real life, but she'd shown it to me many times in dreams, nightmares where I'd find her gaping at me with her blue eyes, water pouring from her mouth. I'd wake up, sweating.

I pictured us in the boat. Cotton and Emery at the oars.

Pete leaning forward at the front to get a better view. I was at the back, making sure we didn't tip over. How close had we come? Maybe within ten metres, it was hard to say. Close enough to know what we were looking at.

Who could say what forensic tools had been put to use back then? It was early days, and the fact that the body had been somewhat inaccessible must have made securing the scene difficult. But then, it also limited who could have had access to the middle of the lake. Lakes are like riverbanks and coastlines, they shift in shape like moods with the change of seasons. We weren't looking at the same lake at all.

We left the shore and headed back into the village. Harry's house remained empty, and the garden was overgrown. The professor's place was also looking quite bedraggled. Emery's house was thankfully shielded from the road by a tall hedge. Pete's old place looked smaller than I remembered it, with a little wooden gate that he must have towered over by the time he left home. My childhood home was the same, but different. I wondered if there was another little boy in the room I'd had, with posters of his own on the walls and bashed up cars parked on the bookshelf. It gave me an odd sensation, like maybe I'd never left that place, and, in some ways, I was still there, reading my collections of books and daydreaming about adventure.

That's the thing with children, they adore the idea of mystery and adventure, while, as adults, everything in society encourages us to stay away from it, to tamp down our imaginations and to toe the line with whatever society expects from us. That's why I loved reading. Or one of the reasons, anyway. You could be sitting on a train with your book, and no one would guess you'd be on some flight of fancy, lost in a world conjured up with words, a world created inside your own head but more real in that moment than the one in which you were present.

I could picture the stairs in that house, the little table next to the front door with the telephone on it, the numbers of friends and local businesses scrawled into a notebook for quick reference. Even the feel of the carpet and the smell of the kitchen were alive to me. It's unsettling to see a place like that, to know it's no longer yours.

Leila had seen enough. She was quite pensive on the way back to Blacksea, looking out the window as we curved across the hills. The clouds were magnificent, though. Huge, rolling masterpieces with vivid white edges and foreboding dark centres. The kinds of clouds that revealed massive faces and shapes before drawing them back in on themselves. Thunder, building. The deep green of the grass glowed with a luminosity that seemed to be stronger than the sun itself, the reflection of its rays rivalling the source.

CHAPTER SIXTEEN

Hook a brother up?

That note played on my mind. The exhortation to remember the past was something I'd kicked against for decades. The frustration at never getting to the bottom of the body in the lake tainted all the memories I'd had of the time. I'd done some reading about childhood trauma and its effects on memory, so I thought there could be some value in chatting to my brothers. They were both older than me and hadn't been present throughout the ordeal since they'd both enrolled at universities a distance away and weren't living in Lakeside.

Aiden and Ryan. We'd been given Irish first names, my parents opting to honour a branch of the family tree that we never climbed - we weren't taken to Ireland on holiday as children and my parents didn't have accents, since neither of them had been born there or grown up in the country. My brothers were born a year apart, almost what you could term Irish twins - when kids are born too close together - and they were four and five years older than me. We got on alright, but their bond was closer to each other than with me.

They'd eventually settled in different towns, cobbled

together their own lives with homes, wives and children. When I met up with them, we got on fine, although neither of them could fathom how I'd managed to stay on for so long in the bookshop, single and seemingly unchanged.

I called Aiden up, and he suggested we meet for lunch at the cricket club where he was a member.

We hugged, shook hands and looked at each other, appraising how the years had affected us.

"Is that grey in your beard, Aidy?" I'd started to find a couple of sneaky grey hairs in my own mop of hair, so seeing him was like a premonition of sorts.

"We're not getting any younger, boyo", he said "I've been thinking about what you mentioned on the phone, so what I'll try to do is let you in on as much as I can remember from back in the day. It'll be like a stream of consciousness thing, though, because I can't remember exact timelines. That okay?".

I nodded.

"Right. 1975, here we come. I was away, first year at uni. So was Ryan, only he was second year. We got a call from mum saying there was a body found in the village and maybe I needed to come home and check on you, because you'd been the one who'd found it. I was distracted by my first real girlfriend, she was almost living with me full time, then. I popped down to Lakeside, though, met up with some old friends, spent some time at the pubs, asked around for as much info as I could get.

From what I recall, you seemed quite normal and not upset at all. I remember chatting to your friends, too. The tall one? Yeah, that's right, Peter. He wasn't phased, either. In fact, he seemed to enjoy the notoriety it gave you kids. Cotton was nuts, as far as I remember, although nothing as crazy as he'd get later on! He seemed to think he was a player - he came up to me (I'll never forget it) in an overcoat that looked like he'd borrowed from his dad and said "Hook a brother up?". It turned out he wanted weed. It wasn't that easy to get back then, and besides, he was still a kid. No way I was going to let the genie out of that bottle by giving him drugs. I think Pete sorted him out in the end, he didn't ask me a second time. Your other friends were just a bit young and nerdy. Shy kids, really, with nothing to say. A bit like you."

That much I knew, but it was interesting to hear his perspective. I accepted that he didn't understand my frame of mind at the time and that he'd been so dismissive.

He continued: "All the other kids were football mad, but not you and your friends. Anyway, I also asked around about the body itself, and there wasn't much to tell. After the initial flurry, it went quiet really quickly. There were a couple of high-profile murders that happened soon after your body was found, but those were in London, or nearby, so maybe they were easier to keep alive as news stories, I just don't know. I also looked at any archaeological digs nearby. I think Pete had the same idea: we went to a few together, actually, but no one seemed to be missing and all the artefacts were accounted for. That's odd, I just had a flashback. That pretty girl, the one you liked for a while, she was like my shadow, turning up at the same places. Angela? Andrea?"

"Amelia?"

"Yep, that's the one. I mean, I had Fiona back at the flat, so I wasn't looking to get mixed up with someone, especially when she was probably underage, then. She was a regular Nancy Drew, though. Notebook, camera and everything. Anyway, after a couple of weeks, I had to go back home and didn't think of it again. The whole thing just slipped off everyone's radar".

"That's it?"

"It was a long time ago, mate. I suppose it was a much bigger deal for you, and I'm sorry I wasn't there at home to cheer you up. Even more so for not popping back recently with everything that's been going on."

I let him know it was all good between us, and we had a great time talking about films, music and nonsense, correcting each other on things misremembered about our childhood.

Ryan was less forthcoming, suggesting that he'd not be able to remember that far back, and also that he was busy trying to get his business back on track after a setback, so he'd not be able to get away. That was typical, but I held no resentment. We each had our own paths to follow.

It was curious, I'd forgotten about Aiden coming home to help out. I suppose I'd been caught up in the events and had tunnel vision, seeing only what I wanted to see. I found it remarkable, too, that even my brother had known to check out the local digs, and that Pete had, too. I was mostly drifting around town over that period, as if I could process something that enormous with every turn of my bicycle wheels. It didn't occur to me that I could fit into the spaces where adults trod. I'd had no idea that Amelia was doing some sleuth work, either. In a village, you become so familiar with the faces you see, you don't always take note of what they're doing, especially if you're a self-involved teenager.

The events of recent weeks were a reminder that you really can't go home again as an adult; that any attempt to insert yourself into your childhood memories is impossible. The people you knew as a child have all either died, moved away or grown up, mostly in ways that you could never have imagined as a child. The alternative would be for the world to be held in suspension, a Neverland of infantilisation, held captive to memory. The tragedy of death does just that, however, closing off the books on a person's life story. They don't get to add any more pages or edit the existing ones. Three dimensions become two.

Back at the shop, Lucien reminded me about the box of documents I'd put aside from the Professor. Lucien wasn't sure where to put them, but he knew I disliked it when things were moved without me knowing about it. I took everything upstairs and spread it out.

It took a few hours to scan my way through all the old folders and booklets. There were copies of theses and dissertations, even a few newspaper, magazine and journal articles that had been stuck to cardboard backing. I was looking for any images that represented artefacts with shells. The shells I'd seen were the kinds with spiralled centres, fairly easily added to a thong or even sewn onto clothing. The paperwork didn't differentiate, so I had to skip through plenty of documents featuring mussel shells and scallops. There were some that looked about right: periwinkles, whelks and conchs, so I stuck to those, although I'd never paid much attention to the different kinds you could find on local beaches. Finally, I found one that was exactly right, and it took way longer than it should have: this shell is, quite literally, known as the Necklace Shell, or *Euspira catena*. It was described as being common around the coast and on sandy beaches.

Like Leila's imaginary murder wall, I needed to create some kind of order to the appearance of the shells within the context of the murder and all of the people associated with that, including me and my friends.

CHAPTER SEVENTEEN

The velvet fingers of a ghost

The first meaningful appearance of the shells was, naturally, on the leather thong tied around the neck of the Lady in the Lake.

Then there was the dig Harry had mentioned, in which a treasure trove of shell artefacts had turned up. A dig that turned out to be one of many such digs, with this region becoming renowned for the shells associated with prehistoric finds.

That last item had been closely followed by Harry's murder, an event that included the presence of shells inside his throat and stomach. This after he'd said he'd had a few theories he'd wanted to explore.

It wasn't a linear timeline, but the body in my own cellar had turned out to be resting on shells and sporting a shell ankle bracelet, although the entire scene had been an ancient one, with remains that had been in place for centuries.

The last instalment of the shell saga had been the one that came with the note labelled Harald M. Berg, along with a handful of ancient pictures of us as kids and a single shell.

As I wrote these notes down, it felt like Shelley was beside me, looking over my shoulder to check that I'd not missed any important details. I could almost feel her cool breath on my neck, the brush of her hair against my face as it caught the breeze from an open window. I could smell the heavy scent of the lake, the vegetation that was decomposing at the banks and the breeze that blew the smells of bracken down from the tops of the hills.

The shell moments weren't as strange as they'd seemed. The ancient roots of shell artefacts made sense, given that the area was known for such findings and that the coast was no doubt closer in those days than it is now. I wasn't sure where Blacksea got its name from, but that alone hinted that the land was in partnership with the ocean around these parts for hundreds of years. It was likely that early settlers had accessed the sea as a means of getting supplies and fish delivered or, just like us, to enjoy time at the beach.

What made the shells out of place were the notes: *"remember the past its still here"*, and the one with Harry's name on it, not to mention the shells found in his throat.

Even if there hadn't been a connection to the body at the lake, someone, somewhere was making a connection. The question was, why didn't they want anyone to know their identity?

There were now three missing identities: the killer, the person sending us messages and Shelley herself. Perhaps the first and second were the same person, I couldn't tell.

Leila and I caught up later that same day. She'd been working on a county-wide case that I didn't know too much about. It involved a poaching syndicate that had been setting traps and catching local wildlife. They were closing the net on a suspect, but it turned out he'd done a runner, leaving behind some hand-drawn maps, lethal-looking traps and a pile of animal corpses. That's all she'd tell me, and that's about all I wanted to hear, anyway. She was pretty good at keeping her job to herself, and I didn't mind. When she was with me; she made an effort to be fully present and I liked to make sure I did the same. The result was a deep bond with plenty of passion but also a warmth, an intimacy that we couldn't have imagined before we got together.

She'd tell me exactly what was on her mind, as long as it wasn't job related. That caught me off guard, but it also taught me to speak my mind so that we were on an equal footing. Mostly we'd have fun talking about some plans that involve travelling, or we'd laugh about the strange requests I'd get in the bookshop.

Leila had grown up a few towns away, close enough to know the area and its quirks, but not quite enough to be fully accepted by the community. No one knew her parents or her background, and she'd not gone to school with anyone local, either. In fact, she'd headed up north after leaving school and then decided to switch careers and become a cop after a friend of hers had died of a drug overdose in the late eighties, heroin started to gain a foothold in nightclubs. I knew from experience as a spectator that heroin was the fast track to problems, having watched a few friends and hangers on back when I'd been a musician. The honeymoon phase with H was way too brief, while the survival stage was tenuous. The shocking truth of it was that it was massive in the industry at the time, and it spread rapidly to general entertainment venues, too. Leila's friend hadn't been a heavy user, she'd just been one of those unfortunates whose constitution (and possibly the strength of whatever she'd taken) wiped her out one night when they should have just been having fun.

As a result, Leila was absolutely opposed to drugs of any sort and was determined to keep them out of the local towns and villages. She'd tracked Cotton during his stay at the inn but hadn't managed to get to the point where she could get a warrant or an opportunity to arrest or search him. I got the strong impression that she disliked him immensely, but he was like that, the coriander version of a personality: enigmatic or reviled.

She seemed somewhat placated when I suggested that he was off the junk these days, but the never-ending saga of addiction means that addicts generally carry that aura of suspicion over their heads. Most recovering addicts accept this as part of their lot, the journey of humility that they need to walk, post-addiction.

I wondered briefly if Shelley had been into drugs; whether that had anything to do with her death. The toxicology report at the time didn't indicate anything, though, but if she or whoever she hung out with had been associated with drugs, that would have been a step closer to a murkier world of criminality, possibly violence.

I knew for sure that Harry never touched the stuff. He'd always had mild health issues. Not enough to cripple him, but enough to give him a pathological approach to life that didn't have room for drugs. My guess is that he was fatalistic and that he suspected that if he ever experimented, he'd be the first to drop dead as a result. Emery I wasn't sure about, but he seemed to be able to create an ebullient mood on the strength of his own passion for music. He was spiritual long before he got religion, but drugs weren't part of his personal epiphany, apart from the occasional joint when he'd been younger.

Leila's professional demeanour was unlike her personal one. When she shed her uniform, her true nature would blossom, a warmth that was endearing and disarming. She barely realised the disparity in her two characters, she just seemed to put on an all-business character when at work and a pleasure-seeking one when at home. Some people are chameleons, they absorb their environments to fit in perfectly. I enjoyed being Leila's camouflage, we wore each other like our own private uniforms.

She was full of surprises, too: one evening, she produced a ukulele from a bag she'd brought round and spent the night singing to me, her gentle voice filling in the gaps between her playing.

Another time, she'd revealed to me that she'd been a competitive swimmer in her youth. That made sense to me, I was so caught up in her presence that she seemed like liquid

beauty that could vanish if I tried to hold on to her too tightly.
Life wasn't bad: for a moment. It was wonderful.

CHAPTER EIGHTEEN

The Sting

It was summer, a few visitors to town enjoying country getaways. I liked them, since they'd pop into the quaint bookshop, buy novels to read on holiday (that they'd never finish). I also stocked some newspapers now that I wasn't likely to turn up on the front pages - it seemed distasteful to sell stories about one's self - and I'd sit outside the shop on a chair with my coffee, reading a few of them.

"UK National Arrested In Sting Operation". A headline caught my eye. There was a photograph accompanying the story that made me spill my coffee onto my lap. He was attempting to cover his face with a scarf and a rolled up newspaper, but his outline was unmistakable: it was Pete.

The article declared that the alleged suspect had been caught trying to dupe a woman out of her inheritance in Italy. The victim's brother had alerted authorities after he'd received notification from the bank that unusual activities were taking place on their shared account. The woman hadn't been harmed and had given a detailed description of the conman, who had been arrested in a set up by the victim in which the police, posing as bankers, had agreed to meet Pete at his hotel, where he was posing as the victim's lawyer.

After the experience with Harry and Emery, I no longer felt confusion when my previously held opinions of people turned out to be wrong. It made sense that Pete could be a con artist, if he chose to. He was good looking, intelligent, and capable. He'd always had a knack for getting along with people, particularly women, with whom he held an affinity. It didn't hurt that he wore suits that made him look like he'd stepped off the photo shoot for a fashion catalogue.

Leila and I read the follow-up stories with interest. Pete had denied everything, claiming that the woman in question was mentally ill and that she'd just forgotten that she'd asked him for investment advice. It seemed plausible, despite the sting operation that had been set up by the woman's wealthy brother.

Just a week later, according to reports, he'd managed to avoid being locked up and had made a daring escape, via boat, into the Mediterranean. He'd distracted the officers while on a visit to the courts and had melted into the crowds.

He was wanted.

It was around that time that the final envelope was delivered. This time, to me, at the bookshop.

I was sent book proofs quite frequently from publishers, so I didn't always open up envelopes that seemed to be related to business. It took me a couple of days to get to this one, addressed to me using my first name only. That was unusual, but it could have been a publisher looking to sell their titles while appearing to be friendly with me. Inside, a short note, once again, and another shell. "Almost" was the only word on the note. It was frustrating getting these hints but no clues that could make any sense in relation to the Lady in the Lake cold case.

Lucien was making tea when he noticed me squinting at the note. He dug the envelope out of the bin, where I'd tossed it, absent-mindedly. "Finn, mate," he said, "did you not see this?". He pointed at the top of the envelope. A postage stamp with a face on it, I had no idea whose, and then an ink stamp in another language.

"It's Spanish, I reckon", he declared, holding it at arm's length towards the light so that the shadow of his beret didn't get in the way.

And it was.

Barcelona.

Amelia.

CHAPTER NINETEEN

Time travel

Spain was a tricky country to contact from abroad, especially if you don't speak Spanish. In this case, contacting Barcelona might just as easily connect you with someone speaking Catalan on the phone. While I could get by enough in Spanish to read a menu or find my way around an airport, I wasn't a conversational speaker.

Barcelona had enjoyed a huge volume of publicity in the run-up to the Olympics a few years earlier and then during the event itself. I'd considered going to watch the athletics, but the idea of being crammed in with all the other spectators had made me decide against it, although I had enjoyed a week-long break there another time, joining smaller crowds to gasp at the *Sagrada Familia* and taking a wander around *Parc Guell* to see Gaudi's inspired mosaics.

I'd always felt an affinity for the place, since Amelia had made a home there, it seemed like it would be easy to get on a plane to find out more about the note and the shell. Worst case scenario, I'd enjoy a summer break on the coast, eating tapas and people watching.

Lucien was fine with it, offering to stay at my place and watch the house, feed the cat and open up the shop. Leila wasn't a hundred percent convinced.

"You want to go and visit your ex-girlfriend in Barcelona?" Her tone was icy, and, when she put it like that, I could see why she wouldn't be thrilled about the idea. Barcelona sounded exotic and summery, the perfect ingredients for a person to fall in love.

"She's not just an ex, she's happily married to a Spanish chap; Tomás, I think his name is. I just can't get to the heart of the information I need from here in Blacksea. I think we should both go, see what we can find out and maybe enjoy a mini break at the same time. I don't think she wants to talk on the phone, otherwise why the cloak-and-dagger approach with envelopes and hints?".

"Yeah, you've made that point, but you're not a detective, there's not much you can do, even if she turned out to be a homicidal maniac herself. Especially if she turned out to be a homicidal maniac".

Leila made a strong case. I'd been about as close as I ever wanted to get to homicide in all its guises, but the tantalising idea of finally achieving closure was too much to resist.

After we had a rational discussion that lasted way too long, including too many sentences that sounded a lot like apologies from me, Leila said she'd go. Her reversal on wanting to go was so sudden that it took me aback.

"Alright, Finn, let's go".

I was still trying to convince her, so I almost missed what she'd said. "Really? What changed there?"

"I've remembered that there's a connection we've got in Barcelona working at Interpol. He's English and worked with me when I was just starting out. He might have access to more information. Besides, I've been trained in the art of accessing information that people may not want to share".

I was careful not to point out that while my historical

connection there was annoying her, it was okay for her to meet up with some international supercop.

We'd matured as a couple.

We set up the travel arrangements and I left the keys with Lucien, who waved goodbye as TS wrapped her sleek tail around his legs.

It amused me that Barcelona was so close, it was easier to fly there than to drive to Scotland. Every time I was able to travel to other countries in Europe, I'd be baffled about why I didn't do it enough. Almost any weekend of the year, I could be enjoying croissants in Paris, or pasta in Florence with just a wave of my credit card at the airport.

The flight was fully booked, though, it being high season. The airport in Barcelona is just a short cab ride out of the city centre, so you get a brief look at the city and the hills that surround it, like a much, much bigger version of Blacksea. The sun was out but we'd chosen to get the early morning flight so it wasn't brutally hot just yet. I'd picked a small hotel in the heart of the tourist district in *Las Ramblas*, within walking distance of the beach and also the old sections of town in the Gothic Quarter.

We took a stroll past pavement cafes and tapas bars, and I think Leila started warming to the place. Our maps set us apart as visitors, but the locals were friendly enough, offering us tastes of cured meats, pastries and breads and a lilting *"Ola"* as we walked. Flags were hanging from plant-covered balconies on endless streets with apartments above and shops below. Locals rode scooters everywhere, from home to work, women sliding their bikes to a stop in a row of other bikes, taking off their helmets and shaking their hair free, back in shape. Taxis and bicycles jostled for space in the wide roads and pedestrians darted for cover with their prams and dogs.

It wasn't hard to imagine moving my entire store here, or perhaps just opening another branch that I could visit whenever I chose. You know a city has you by the heart when you start wondering how easily you could sink roots there. Amelia must have felt exactly that feeling years before as she made the change from visitor to local.

The temptation to embrace the geographic cure is always there in times of stress: had enough? Just get out. I had an extensive armchair travel section in the shop - an entire literary genre written by people who had done just that, aimed at people for whom the romance of travel was either a dream or a goal. You could buy a book and find yourself drifting away on a daydream in Central America or, vicariously, tasting the street food in a crowded market in Southeast Asia. There would be vagabonds and heroes throughout these adventures, their escapades bringing the travel experience to life in technicolour.

If you've ever wanted to strike up a conversation with someone but you weren't sure how to do it, you could ask them to choose between a desert island or a forest cabin in the mountains and to explain why. The sheer romance of a place is brought about by the scents, sounds and potential experiences you may encounter, or the promise of peace and tranquillity.

We spent a couple of days wandering the city, holding hands and slowly becoming oblivious to the situation back home. This entrancing place with its churches and rolling hills facing a massive port abutted by incredible beaches was a haven. I even tried muttering a few Spanish phrases, but the locals took pity on us, either using abundant body language to help us or a few words of English to prove that they were more capable than us of communicating.

On the third day, we woke up early, knowing that the time had come to get to work. I'd paid a hotel worker to find Amelia's number in the local directory, which they'd done, so I called to set up a meeting.

"Amelia!" I went for a tone that sounded happy and carefree. "It's Finn. Lakeside Finn".

That sounded like a villain's name, and I heard her draw a sharp breath on her end of the line.

"Finn... how did you get this number?"

"I have my ways". I laughed. "I'm here with a friend (Leila

looked at me sharply) in Barcelona, actually. I'd love to see you while we're here".

"I don't know if that's the best idea. Tomás is away on business right now, in Chile."

"It's important, Meel". I used my pet name for her and felt Leila's gaze on the back of my neck. "We're only here for a short time and I think we need to discuss something, something I think you'd like to share with me". I was getting the sense that she'd rather not, but if those notes had been hers, then this was her chance.

The call went silent for a full half minute before she responded. "You know what, let's do it, it's the right thing to do".

We set up a time and a place and I hung up the phone. I was shaking. "She'll meet us at three this afternoon at the park at the top of the *Montjuïc* Cable Car. Both of us".

Leila was quiet, but we were hoping to make some headway in the case, so it was, finally, a step that may provide some tangible results rather than theories.

She'd brought a small tape recorder to capture the conversation but promised to get permission before using it. As the morning progressed and we made our way across the city, she seemed to become more professional, gaining a tension across her shoulders and a frown that wouldn't leave her face. DI Stanbury was in action.

The short cable car trip lifted us above the city toward the hilltops, over the trees and buildings and offering a panoramic view of the coast and the grids of city blocks that stretched out as far as we could see.

Amelia was waiting at the top.

We hugged, she greeted Leila with some warmth, and I noted the slight accent she'd picked up. She was tanned, the brown of her skin accentuated by the light blue of the dress she was wearing. Her hair was tied up.

There was tension in the air.

We found a bench away from the crowds with their backpacks and cameras and sat, each of us waiting for the other to open the lid to this Pandora's Box of a conversation.

"Finn." Amelia opened. "You know, I've got so many fond memories of our friendship growing up. Leila, don't worry, everything I'm about to say is absolutely in the past, or, at least, that's where I want it to stay".

I nodded. I was grateful that she'd both noticed that Leila was more than a friend to me and that she would like the reassurance. Showed my palms to her to let her continue.

"That village was always too small for me, for us. For anyone, really. But especially for me. It felt claustrophobic. Then, all at once, I couldn't spend another summer there."

"1975," I said. "For me, that's where it all started".

"That's true, but it's also only part of the truth. Here's what happened to me, while you were all caught up in those events".

She laid out a carefully curated version of what had happened, how it had drawn her in and, finally, why she'd been unable to let it alone, even after all these years.

The discovery of the body in the lake had disturbed her in ways she couldn't express. She'd spent months, just as we had, trying to make sense of the case and doing some amateur detective work that achieved nothing.

The entire town had been drawn in and then left in suspense as there were no clues beyond what we already knew. It took a couple of years before she came across anything that might hint at what really happened.

Just before we'd rekindled a friendship and had a brief relationship of sorts, she'd met someone else. He'd tried his best to win her over, but she was deliberately cautious. This person gave her what she termed a "bad vibe" She went on to explain that it wasn't just that he was creepy, but it was like he carried with him a shadow that only she could see. Like the darkness he tried to conceal was leaking, attaching itself to him.

He was persistent, and they'd tried one, awful date. He could tell by the end of the evening that she wasn't happy and became cool, aloof. When he dropped her off at home, he looked her in the eyes, reached into his pocket and asked her to hold out her hand.

"We're bonded together, you and me, Amelia", he'd said, placing something in her hand.

It had been a leather thong, a bracelet strung with small shells.

He'd continued: "We're a part of the story of this village and everything that goes on. I got this from one of the digs up near Wilham; it reminds me that we share everything here. The good, the bad."

Amelia said that at that point she'd been shaking with fear and had left his car, stuttering about having to be up early, only realising that she still held the bracelet after she got into the house. It was the last time they went out together.

By the time she'd got through this part of the conversation, she was crying.

"Then you and I got together, and that was lovely for a while, but I had to go. Every time I saw him, it felt like his eyes were burning holes into me. His superficial charm had turned into a rage that only I could see. And everywhere you went, there he was".

Charm. Even as she said it, I felt a chill down my spine. It was a village, by definition: small, and it wasn't hard to isolate the person she was talking about. My friend, Pete. The gangly child who'd become a tall man with a sense of style that was more big city than small town. The man who could seduce with a glance. I'd seen it.

"Pete." I wasn't sure what her confession meant.

"Yes. Pete. What he shows you is not what he shows other people. Every moment with him is like watching a horror film and knowing that something bad is going to happen. The weird thing is, he wasn't nasty, violent or even threatening. In fact, the sweeter he tried to be, the more my skin crawled".

She wiped her face with her sleeve. "I'd come across him and your brother while we were following the pathetic leads that existed around that cold case. I'd see him watching me. He was always in that grocer's van, and he turned up at every corner

I was exploring. Eventually, I stopped looking, mainly because I couldn't stand to see him anymore".

"I sent you those shells and that message with your names because this has been a thorn in my side for decades. I have no idea if he did anything, especially... *that*, but when you live with a maybe in your head, it just niggles away. Then, you found another body, and it made me want to intervene, but I couldn't risk everything I've built here, my life, my marriage. I figured that you, your childhood gang, would understand that this had never gone away."

Her reaction to her own story had been quite astonishing to see. She'd cried, looked at me with desperation visible in her eyes, pleading with me to see what she saw.

"Do you think..." I couldn't finish the sentence. "I mean, we were just kids..."

"That's the problem, Finn. The whole village lost its innocence that summer. Sure, he could just be an awful person, a manipulator, but what if... what if... it's the 'what if's' that need to be answered".

Leila had been listening, not saying a word. She spoke, finally: "Amelia, you're brave to be sharing this. My professional opinion is that you'd not be called as a witness if what we think happened, happened, and there's an arrest. Your gut feelings are completely valid, but not much good in court".

Amelia nodded, sniffed.

That gave an air of finality to the conversation. As we left, Amelia hugged me again and pressed the remains of a bracelet with half a dozen shells on it into my hand, closing my fingers on it. She seemed to take a deep breath, as if she'd been set free from a lifetime of anxiety. We headed back to the Cable Car station and drifted back down to the city with its flocks of pigeons and seagulls.

The flight home felt like it took too long, with the light conversation we'd enjoyed while exploring turning into extended periods of silence.

Back in Blacksea, there was work to be done, but Leila

wasn't keen on me interfering, she'd put in a formal request to investigate the cold case, and my involvement put her judgement at risk, or, at least, that's how it could appear to her senior officer. We agreed to spend some time apart, but I'd say that she agreed more than I did. I was annoyed to be sidelined.

Amelia's revelation in part didn't produce a conclusive answer, though.

Even if the shells turned out to be the same as the ones on the Lady in the Lake, all that meant was that Pete had managed to acquire similar shells.

It meant that I'd have to revisit my memory banks, creating a timeline that was less pockmarked with holes, one that had a renewed perspective.

That day we'd found the body; Pete had led us to it. He'd not shown any kind of fear or unusual behaviour. I could still picture him cruising down the road on his bike with his arms folded.

His reaction to the find had been to call the police; again, not something you'd expect from a guilty person. He'd tried his best to solve the case along with all of us and had been one of the first to agree to join me in this latest debacle with the body in the basement.

The first indication that he may not be as innocent as I'd imagined came with the revelations that he may have conned a woman in another country, although the pictures he'd sent me made him seem relaxed and calm, surrounded by a different woman each time, although each woman had an eerily similar expression, as if they'd found a valuable antique in a junk shop, a secret they knew that they didn't want anyone else to find out.

As far as I could tell, he was on a boat somewhere in the Mediterranean, staying clear of the authorities.

CHAPTER TWENTY

One day we'll look back
on this and laugh

My mental health was in the toilet. The breadth of betrayal I'd experienced lately had left me feeling battered and sorry for myself. What I found confusing was that I'd largely managed to move on from the Lady in the Lake and the years with the band in my late teens. I could have continued creating a pleasant life in town working in the bookshop and never spared another thought to childhood friends. It had been my own doing, to re-invite them back into my life and to set that monster in motion that had resulted in tragedy and disappointment. It had prompted the police to investigate us and our association with a cold case but then also connected the dots with current misdeeds (or suspected ones) on behalf of Harry and Emery. Cotton hadn't really changed too much, he's always been a Tasmanian devil of a character, but he'd also managed to avoid extensive prison time. When Leila had mentioned Pete's connection to three assault cases, I'd just assumed they were to do with his work in the betting shop, that he was used as an enforcer of some sort. It never occurred to me that he might pose a danger to women or, worse still, that he may have hurt three of them.

I made a trip to the Primrose Inn, hoping to see the woman who'd worked at the front desk while I was staying there. She was only scheduled to do the late shift that afternoon, so I ended up having lunch there, a depressing meal that would've tasted completely like bad decisions and regret had I not drowned my plate in gravy.

There was a jukebox in the pub, placed a little too close to the dart board, but no one was using that at the moment so I checked out the selection. The thing about jukeboxes, they always seem to stock the same songs, exactly the playlist you'd expect a pub band to play, too. This one was no different, with some light rock, ballads and a few real old-time-y classics. I chose one. Doris Day singing Dream a Little Dream of Me. The record slid into place and crackled to life, her lilting voice a juxtaposition of sweetness and confusion.

As the song faded, the owner put his head around the glass-windowed door. "She's here". I headed for the foyer with its bedraggled pamphlets advertising things to do in the area.

Louise. That was her name. It said so on her lapel badge.

"Louise, can I get you a coffee?" She said yes, she could chat for a few minutes. The hotel was empty, as far as I could tell.

I asked about that night with Pete. How he'd treated her. She blushed for the briefest moment and dismissed the evening.

"He was a bit disappointing, actually. I thought he'd be a bit wilder but he turned out to be quite dull. It was over in a few minutes. In fact, he seemed to lose interest the minute his door was closed. Embarrassing." She looked at the door as if worried that the owner would peek in.

"But you felt… safe?"

"I didn't feel unsafe, but it was stupid of me to have gone ahead with it. He avoided eye contact with me the rest of the time he stayed here, making me feel even worse. That was cruel, but I blamed myself and just tried to ignore him".

She got up after that, cleared the coffee cups and headed into the back office. It sounded like she was being quite angry with some files, slamming the door to the big, grey cabinet with some force.

This wasn't just a cold case, it was positively frozen. Each avenue I explored seemed to add another layer of nothing, diluting the basic facts even further.

That evening, though, everything changed.

Leila let herself into the house through the closed shop and came upstairs to see me. TS circled her legs, brushed against her as she stood in my doorway. Purred.

"Something's come up," she said, "but I can't say too much at this point. You'll need to trust me, but we're making progress".

I didn't know whether she meant progress into the cold case or into tracking Pete down. It was like someone hinting at a surprise but never letting you know what the surprise was.

"Reason I came here, Finn, is that you may get some media hassling you again. It would be best if you went with *'no comment'* at this stage. We may not know what happened with Harry, but we can be sure that there's a slight danger that you could be targeted."

That was no comfort at all. Targeted - the word made me think of snipers on rooftops or bombs planted under car seats - over-dramatic for sure, but then Harry had been murdered with ease, despite him being on high alert given his job.

"Well, thanks, Leila, I feel really safe, now".

"Ah, don't be peevish, Finn. Just keep your eyes open and watch yourself with the press". She left again.

I barely noticed headlines anymore, but I could do without being in them. *"Bookseller Dies In Murder Mystery Come True"* was not a headline I cared to feature in.

The actual headlines over the next two days turned out to be something I'd never have been able to predict.

"Could This Be Her? Cold Case Victim Identity Unlocked".

"Lake Body Identified 20 Years Later".

"DNA Reveals Murder Truth After Two Decades".

The short version of the story behind the headlines was that private investigators had been recruited by Cotton to explore the DNA option. The royalties of our music had produced a tidy windfall that covered extensive tests, tests that had reached international offices. The Lady in the Lake had origins in Poland and, after months of searching, the investigators had managed to isolate a couple of missing person's cases that seemed to hold potential. A few more tests for compatibility with family members and they'd announced, with relative certainty, the victim's name.

Kaja. Kaja Trojak.

Her name was displayed beside an old photograph.

She was young, beautiful. Blonde hair with a fringe in that distinctive 70s style, eyes looking over the photographer's left shoulder as if seeing a plane flying overhead.

The information given was scant, but it gave a brief snapshot into this person who followed me like a ghost for so long. Shelley. Kaja.

Kaja had grown up in Lubniewice, Poland. A little picture captured it as a tiny hamlet straddling two lakes. She'd spent her school years there before heading to England in 1975 at the age of seventeen to find work, possibly as an au pair or a maid. That was as much as her parents knew. They were both dead, but an old missing person's file had been kept in the back room of the local police station. Once DNA searches became useful in the identification of missing persons, older missing persons files were moved to a larger storage complex in Warsaw, making it easier to compare with local and international queries.

A couple of paragraphs that summed up her life. Barely anything at all.

I had wept while reading them, a lifetime of emotions overwhelming me as I imagined her waving goodbye to her mum and dad after they dropped her at the station. I hoped she'd known enough English to get by, but I also knew that Polish people were treated badly then by locals. A swathe of immigrants to the UK after the Second World War and during the Communist era had allowed British people to use them as cheap labour in relatively thankless jobs, with their ethnic origins becoming something of a dismissive slur. Communication between the two countries would have been difficult, it was unlikely that her parent's local authorities had even been approached with a request to identify a body.

She'd found her way to our region, maybe moving with other migrants as they worked the farmlands during planting and harvest time. It was unlikely that she'd been moonlighting as an academic on an archaeological dig. She was vulnerable, and, as was ultimately proven, tragically disposable.

It was also possible that she'd been forced to turn to sex as a means of getting by, her dreams of learning English while working as an au pair fading with each passing day of unpaid rent. So many missing persons that fit her profile turned out to be dismissed, with no robust investigation taking place. There had been several murders that year, and still more women who went missing. Their stories included women who were dressed and ready to start their evening shift at work but they'd never arrived, women who'd last been seen getting into cars outside nightclubs, women who had vanished leaving their handbags and even their keys at home on the kitchen table. What seemed like an entire generation of them.

She wasn't Shelley any longer. She wasn't the Lady in the Lake.

She'd been just a little bit older than me, and she'd never had the chance to grow up, to laugh her way through the carefree 80s and into the 90s.

I wished there were more details in the articles I found, but they focused more on the wonders of DNA identification. None of the articles mentioned me by name, but one or two mentioned Cotton for his fundraising efforts. Harry and Emery were also left out, as was Pete. The media seemed to have tunnel vision, being unable to link different stories to each other. That worked out in my favour. They had alluded to the fact that only the victim's identity had been established using DNA and that there were no clues as to the identity of the killer. The body hadn't yielded any other DNA evidence.

The shock of knowing her identity after so long had knocked me. I suppose I'd only ever seen pictures of her as recorded by the coroner: bruised, dead, inhuman. Just one photo of her with a spark in her eye and hope plainly written across her face helped me to rid myself of the nightmares I'd carried, a corpse endlessly wandering the beaches searching for more shells to add to her necklace but never being able to rest.

I felt ill. The stupidity of that song we'd written and sang felt exploitative. I had to remind myself that we were just too young to handle the situation with any maturity back then but present me was disgusted with younger me. I wanted to call Harry and Emery and let them know, but they'd both gone to their graves in ignorance, as had Kaja's parents.

Closure is a concept that I never grasped. If you viewed life and time as strictly linear, maybe it made sense: Birth-life-death. But if you've lived for a while, you realise that there are convolutions and overlaps. Living people are sometimes dead inside, while the threat of mortality and impending death can inspire people to do more than they've ever done before, to go beyond the boundaries they'd previously set for themselves. Once dead, they seldom stayed dead. In dreams, daydreams and intrusive thoughts, the dead can walk again, speaking blessings and curses into the ears of those left behind. Some people are firm believers in the ways ancestors can impact your current life, and others believe in reincarnation. It's difficult to reduce life to a finite journey if you believe in those things.

It was important to let Amelia know.

I called her, gave her the news and listened as she cried a bit. I'd sent her a faxed copy of the articles, and imagined how she must have felt to see them easing their way out of the fax machine, painstakingly revealing Kaja's face, bit by bit. It wasn't as satisfying as I'd hoped: we knew who she was, but not the circumstances of her death. We were nudging closer, but it was also possible that this could be the end of it all.

Leila was supportive. She understood what it was to see something through, having investigated cases with both outcomes before: resolved or unresolved. She guessed that I was still hoping to see Kaja's killer exposed, and said she'd keep on checking any leads. Her cold case at last had an identity attached to it.

Forgetting any connection to Pete, the possibility remained that her killer was long gone, dead or relocated, maybe locked away in prison.

Twenty years is enough time for a person to get married, have a few jobs, maybe a couple of children. They can lose all their hair or put on fifty kilograms. Grow a beard, shave one off. Any number of physical changes can take place. There never were any eyewitness accounts of the killing, but even if there had been, they'd be completely useless by now. Too much water under the bridge.

CHAPTER TWENTY-ONE

Hacked

At first, I feared that I was becoming paranoid; I'd noticed cars and flashes of people in my peripheral vision. The sensation that I was being watched escalated. Lucien said that it was quite probable that I was being followed, but I knew he liked to spend a lot of time browsing books in the New Age section, a catch-all group of shelves that contained titles on mysticism, conspiracy theories and quasi-spirituality. He wasn't the right person to ask for a balanced perspective, unless you were looking for his opinion on crop circles.

It came to a head one day when a black car with tinted windows skidded to a stop on the gravel outside the shop. Just as Harry had described. Two men got out, again, echoing Harry's description of the encounter. I almost snorted with amusement at the idea they'd try and recruit me for whatever agency they worked for, given that my computer and accounting skills were equally pathetic.

They sat with me as we had coffee downstairs in my new kitchen. Every couple of minutes, Lucien popped his head downstairs to see if I was okay, or just out of curiosity - I couldn't be sure.

"Who's the Lady in the Lake?" one of them asked. I spent a couple of minutes giving them the standard response that we'd found silenced people like that.

They'd already known who she was, I suppose it was some kind of test to see how I'd respond.

"We'd like to talk about your friend, Mr. Berg".

It took a second for me to realise they were talking about Harry, but I nodded for them to go ahead.

"Mr. Berg has worked with us for some years. He was a genius at obtaining information, important information. So much so that losing him has been a huge blow to us".

It felt insensitive of them to state their case like that, since I'd been his friend, likely to have more of an emotional connection to him. Also, it seemed that his work had involved their mandate to expose criminal syndicates, so they could have put him in the line of fire.

"What we've found. Looking deeper into his activities, though, are some details we'd not been aware of."

I shrugged; I knew very little about Harry's side project.

"He was using global networks to access information that would be considered highly confidential. He may even have been in contact with hackers. He was almost certainly writing his own code and encrypting much of what he was storing."

Again, I only understood the vague concepts of coding and computers, although the latest news hinted that soon everyone would be communicating across the world from their own homes via the World Wide Web. I knew this, not from personal experience, but from books being sold to me by reps, but there was very little demand for those kinds of titles; my customers preferred books about nature or cooking, not coding.

"In particular, he seems to have amassed vast quantities of data about criminals around the world. We're not just talking about financial crimes, it seemed like he was particularly interested in homicides and missing persons".

At that point, I gave them a full rundown of how we'd

become embroiled in a cold case and we'd made a pact to resolve it.

"That's just it, it seems like he'd hit on something that was taking place across Europe over the past decade. It could be a trafficking ring, organised crime, it's hard to say at this point. Our speciality is financial crimes and money laundering, but, of course, we'd like to know if he was in over his head in something else and our records have been compromised."

"I don't know enough to help you out here. I'm sorry. I'm disgusted that you may have put his life at risk and exploited his skills; we may not have been close but he didn't deserve to die like that; you should have protected him".

"What's your connection to a Mr. Peter Fryer?".

Oh. That was a name I didn't want to appear next to mine in print, much less in an investigation. I said as much to them.

"His name is repeated so much, we can't see if it's some kind of bug in the system or if Harry was following a lead. The name is mentioned in connection with documents about Spain, France, Italy, Malta and then Central America and Thailand, too. So many countries but no obvious thread that we can make out."

I was thinking about the many, many photos Pete had sent me over the years, the smiling women, so many of them that they almost became anonymous. His grin, his sunglasses and his hat, always tilted to one side.

A sense of dread crept up and down my spine as I realised what these photos might be.

"You know, I hate to say it, but I have no idea what you're talking about", I said.

They were disappointed, but they acknowledged that it was possible I'd never been taken into Harry's confidence.

"We'd like to leave you with these files. They're printouts of what Harry had been working on. Please take a look, there might be a name or a code you recognise".

"Are you sure? I don't want to get stuck into anything that's confidential".

"These files would be meaningless to anyone out of

context, you can do with them as you will without any fear of repercussions".

"What if *I* am the context? Who's going to clean up my body?".

We said our goodbyes, and they left me holding a business card, for when I needed to get in touch with them.

I watched as their car headed slowly back up the road and remembered that odd day, the one where it all began, and the red van we'd seen. Fresh Lamb. Like lamb to the slaughter - that's how I felt.

It seemed like Pete had lured us all into *his* slaughterhouse - a thought I had that turned out to be prescient and terrifying.

I went back into the shop, headed for the shelves. There were only a few books on computing, just basic introductory titles. This subject was largely the province of quiet types who seemed to see something among all the numbers and symbols that the rest of us couldn't. I browsed through the books, but nothing jumped out at me. A thought occurred: if Cotton's fan base had been able to mobilise to uncover Kaja's identity, then maybe they could expose what Harry had been investigating.

Cotton wasn't around at any of the numbers I tried calling him on. Or he wasn't picking up. I wouldn't blame him: considering the trail of death that had taken place, his default paranoia seemed quite justified, I was tempted to go into hiding myself.

Harry's death was bugging me. If his own people hadn't been brought up to speed with what he was doing and, as far as I could gauge, had no part in his death, it meant that there could be another killer on the loose, if not several of them. If I was going to try and uncover what he'd been working on, I was risking going up against this person or group with no protection at all. It seemed right, though. Just like we'd vowed to find out what had happened to the Lady in the Lake, the same no-man-left-behind attitude should apply to our own. Emery's personal conflicts had prevented this ethos from happening in practice, but I still held on to it.

Cotton was too wrapped up in his own complexities, so it looked like it was up to me. As humans, one of the first errors we make is creating unnecessary problems for ourselves. Adding layers that don't need to be there. Problem solving can be as easy as realising this: Maybe I didn't need to enter the murky world of hackers; I could just call the most public coding companies around and ask for their help.

So, I did.

It wasn't easy tracking people down, and the top coders seemed to be away from their desks a lot of the time, opting to work at night when their offices were quieter.

The final solution was the most obvious one: phone the police. I got in touch with the department attached to tech crime and explained my problem.

They responded favourably, since I'd posed the situation like a challenge that they'd need to crack, appealing to their competitive nature. They also asked me to drop off any associated files. That made me nervous, but at least if someone was tailing me, they'd know the information was out of my hands.

I took the long drive into the city with an unfamiliar feeling of serenity. It was going to be out of my hands, up to experts and specialists again. The HQ was a concrete block a few storeys high, a modern building that had been built to house the 'New Police', as they called them, a force working not just the streets but on computers with databases and archived records. That was the plan - there were decade's worth of files to be added to the records, but it was happening fast. Teams of students on their breaks worked there during the holidays to type up the records and file away the originals.

That's why I was hopeful that this new wave of policing could yield some clues from the data Harry had left behind.

I was ushered into a lift and up to the fourth floor, a place that didn't feel like a policing office at all, it felt more like a branch of IBM. Every desk had a computer on it. Sitting at those desks were people whose uniforms seemed to be black t-shirts and trainers.

There was a corner office, I was welcomed in and asked to sit down.

I handed over the information I'd been given, and explained what I hoped to find, and what Harry had been working on. At the last minute, before leaving the house, I'd added all the photos that Pete had sent me from his travels, too. I wasn't why I did that, but it made sense to me to keep any papers and pictures together.

There was a very short man pacing the room behind me, he was quite jittery, almost as much as Cotton when he was strung out. The small guy grabbed at the printouts and his eyes lit up. What to me were as illegible as hieroglyphics were structured codes that he seemed to be able to read with ease. He giggled to himself.

"An accountant, you say? He most assuredly was not just an accountant. Even the most careless glance reveals some highly advanced coding. It will take time, but I think we can make sense of all this. We'll let you know". He sounded like a warlock who'd just found an ancient book of spells he'd been seeking.

He slipped out the door holding the box as if carrying a holy relic into a cathedral, and I made my way back outside.

CHAPTER TWENTY-TWO

Lucien's dream

Back in the village, I spent a few days in the bookshop, making sure that it was making some money at least. Lucien came in most days, although he didn't have a fixed schedule. We'd sit drinking tea, comparing passages in obscure books and relaxing, mostly, helping out customers who came in for a weekend read or for a book club selection.

Lucien had a trick when it came to selling books. I'd only noticed it after listening in a few times to his conversations with customers. He'd grab a book, proclaiming that it was "book of the year" for him, that it had made him weep or laugh out loud. Then he'd say something to the effect of "page 156! I dare you to read that without having an emotional episode". Then he'd quote the text, verbatim.

He was a relatively clever man, but I doubted that he had a photographic memory, so I called him out one day after the customer had left with his recommendations.

"Lucien, that was an impressive sale, I have to say. But I'm curious, what happens on page 157?"

He snort-laughed, spilling his tea on the desk. "I don't

memorise the whole book. Who could bear to do that? I just take one passage and remember which page it's on. Then it's a case of matching the reader with the style of writing".

Ingenious, if a little crafty.

He came in one morning looking a bit worse for wear. He hadn't slept well, he said, proceeding to tell me about a dream he'd had. The dream involved a graveyard emerging in the cellar of the shop, and, from the graves, a host of corpses, all women, all mouthing something he couldn't hear.

That sounded too much like reality to me, although to anyone else it would be a horror story. I saw those kinds of things without even dreaming.

We went down into the cellar together to put his mind at ease. I even knocked on the flooring to demonstrate that it was solid. He calmed down.

"That's why I prefer to read fantasy", he admitted, "You can't confuse reality with men in tights fighting dragons".

I thought back to the two women I'd found, twenty years apart. One, a young Polish woman who'd had a real history with a real family. The other, the remains of a woman who'd likely had a family, too, although her lifestyle would have been quite different. In a sense. They'd emerged from their graves to tell their tales and had been mouthing silent messages to me ever since.

After Leila had let me know about the origins of the body in the basement, I'd read up about bog bodies, a phenomenon that occurred throughout Europe, where bodies were recovered in peat bogs. There were a few in the United Kingdom, and It seemed like I'd been lucky, most of the other ones, once discovered, had prompted exploratory excavations lasting years. Mine had just taken a few weeks, since the body was in a protected building and there was no feasible way of excavating the entire town, most of which was also established on historical bog lands.

What was curious was that bog bodies didn't come with their stories written, so archaeologists and historians were left to surmise how they'd lived and died based on the evidence before them. Some may have been ritual sacrifices, others, murder victims or victims of armed conflict. Some may have been suicides. It made for fascinating reading. I gazed at pictures of them, too. Many seemed to be sleeping, as if they'd simply lain down in the bog and been slowly absorbed into it. Often, they looked as if they'd been cast in bronze: dark, glossy skin and incredible detail, right down to facial wrinkles and fingernails. Their teeth and skeletons, as well as the contents of their stomachs, helped to flesh out their histories. Their clothes, if there were any, were used to date their corpses. Some wore tunics woven from fibres specific to certain regions, while others were clad mostly in leather garments. Many of them had jewellery around their ankles, wrists or necks. Their lives and deaths had been dated (worldwide) at between 8,000 BCE and as recently as the Second World War, so it was possible to be preserved at any time in human history.

It gave me a sense of peace to read out these discoveries in a dispassionate way. It helped to take me out of their stories, making me instead a spectator on a narrative that could never be completed, one that belonged to them, not me. Any guilt I felt lifted as a result.

The hunter doesn't see game as an emotional product of his activities, and the butcher doesn't have feelings about the meat he'll divide into manageable portions. I'd made the mistake of injecting a large portion of emotions and feelings into a situation that could be analysed and annotated as a scientific event instead.

Approaching the body in the basement with this in mind gave me some detachment.

When it came to Kaja's body in the lake, however, I couldn't rid myself of the need to find out more, the need to fill the gaps in her story. She wasn't a ritual sacrifice (I hoped) and she'd not been a victim of war, either. She'd been an ordinary girl doing ordinary things before her life was ended for her near a sleepy village. The war for her had been a social one in which society had branded her the enemy by virtue of her foreign birth and clumsy attempts at speaking a second language.

I was grateful that Lucien's dream had reminded me of a healthier perspective, that I needn't take either death personally, but I could find out more information with self-preservation in place, treating them as dispassionately as a hunter with a rabbit or a butcher with a ham hock. In theory.

The call from the cybercops came in on a Friday. I took the trip out to see them, hopeful that they'd found something. The contact person hadn't wanted to reveal anything over the phone, even their name, so I wasn't even sure if it was a real call or a prank.

Martin, the small man I'd dealt with initially, was red in the face with excitement.

"I can't believe what I've been seeing here. This is history in the making!". For a cop, he was decidedly over the top.

"We've only had our department open since last September and this case, yes, it's a case, has just bought us another decade of funding. It's exactly the kind of work we need to prove what we can do. If only I'd met your Harry - what an absolute genius!".

Harry was a bright spark when it came to numbers. I mean, he'd always handled the band's finances and we had no quarrels about money the way other bands did. But a genius? Not just a "famous drummer", then.

Martin was literally bouncing on the edge of his seat.

"He didn't just write a code, he wrote a code, within a code, on top of another code!"

"Right... I understand". (I didn't).

"Let me dumb... Uh, make it easier for you to get the idea".

Dumb it down. Fair enough.

"He was tracking criminal networks using financial data that was secured by the institutions. We don't have a full profile of what exactly he was doing there, but you can read between the lines; lines of code, that is. It appears that he added an additional layer of search relating to, first of all, archaeological information and then, missing persons across Europe and further afield."

I sat up a bit, that sounded more like something I needed to hear.

"He was able to access data files the minute archived information was added to the system, so he'd set up some sort of self-notification program. But wait, there's more!"

"He'd found significant commonalities in the data and then kept notes in files of his own in a code that he'd written that none of us could understand. It was pure chance that we stumbled across a possible interpretation. One of our data investigators happens to moonlight as a music instructor at the university. Not strictly approved by his bosses, but there you go. His main area of interest is drumming. Now, drumming is often seen as a discipline learned by people who can't read music. Many drummers just put on a pair of earphones and copy what they hear while playing. Max, the instructor I just mentioned, takes a different approach. He's learned drumming in its more formal format, with tablature that's very similar to musical notes. He was the first to recognise that Harry had created computer code based on drum patterns."

I was still struggling to grasp how this all fit together and, if at all, why Harry would go to the effort of concealing his findings.

"Let me summarise. It looks like Harry has uncovered a massive trail of murders across Europe, from the UK as far as Greece. There may even be connected cases in Central America and the Far East. He's annotated hotspots of activity, those commonalities we mentioned. Then he's traced those back to other commonalities. Enough information to give us suspects".

I felt like he wanted to have a "ba-dum-tish!" at the end of his speech to celebrate their success, but I was in awe that Harry had managed to do any of this. It certainly expanded the list of potential perpetrators involved in his death, that's for sure.

Martin waited for me to process what he'd said.

"You also gave us a selection of photographs. I don't see any of Harry's notes referring to those, but we're glad you did.

Of the women featured in those pictures, at least eight of them fit the profiles of the missing persons Harry was tracking. And, naturally, there's the presence of one person throughout. Peter Fryer. Now the prime suspect in what looks like a multinational serial killing case". Martin clapped his hands together. "You just never find this amount of information in one go. It's astounding".

I thanked Martin, who said they'd be putting the investigation into top gear, gathering all the facts and evidence, creating a timeline (or multiple timelines, it seemed) and building their case. He added that while they were grateful for the huge head start, they'd been given, at this point in the life cycle of the case, I'd need to step back. Of course, I agreed, but then I had immediately resolved to continue gathering information of my own.

In Lakeside, at the police station, I took on the role of informant to Leila's detective persona. She was angry with me for taking things to another level with a different branch of the police, but after she realised what they'd achieved, her anger subsided. She knew how important this was to me, and, for the sake of the larger community, she wanted closure, too.

She was just as upset with herself for not picking up anything strange about Pete, for not reading him better and for seeing him as a victim rather than a suspect. She'd known about the assault cases and, in her own mind, she realised she should have been actively investigating him rather than leaving it up to other departments in other cities.

One thing I was grateful for was my obsession with keeping records of everything. After our time in the band, even though Harry had been meticulous with our finances, we still got calls from the Revenue Services. To be fair, many musicians had chaotic financial records: managers disappearing with bankrolls, massive debts accrued on bloated tours with unpaid bills and plenty of dodgy deals done on a cash-only basis. Harry had insisted on record keeping, so I followed suit, making copies of every document that came my way. You'd be amazed to find that even a bill signed by a musician could be stolen by a fan as a memento.

This obsession led to me keeping a record of recent events, too, including copies of the documents and photos I'd dropped off at the cybercrime department.

It was mind-boggling that all those pictures sent to me by Pete were part of some trail he wanted to leave. Was it vanity? It was difficult to see what his motive could be. I went through them another time, along with a sense of dread. Each face could be a missing person. After all these years trying to find out Kaja's story so I could get some closure, I was faced with a whole collection of women whose histories had come to a premature end.

What took us to the next step turned out to be another "Keep It Simple" eureka moment that I had.

CHAPTER TWENTY-THREE

Mirror image

I was going through my collection of murder notes and pictures (not my murder, but the murder or murders) when an idea occurred to me. It took a moment to confirm my thought, but I was right: each picture Pete had sent to me was taken by someone else. Not the various women next to him at different times - the distance was just too far away from them for them to have flipped the camera to face themselves. I'd always assumed that these pictures were taken at pool parties or events where there were a lot of people around and the camera had been handed to someone else after they'd been asked to take a picture of Pete and whomever he was with. These latest revelations that these could be missing women, though, had me wondering who was missing them. Could it be the person on the other side of the camera lens?

That didn't make sense. If you saw one or two photos, you could have made that assumption, but when viewed all together in sequence, you could see that it was the same hand taking the pictures, or the same eye, at least.

Photography is a skill I'd never learned. The pictures I'd tried to take as a kid were generally blurred or they included a large section of my thumb that had covered the shutter. Ryan, my other brother, had enjoyed taking pictures for a while. He'd studied books on photographers, too, enjoying Ansel Adams and Edward Weston's perspectives on landscapes. Ryan enjoyed nature photography - birds, trees, water - since he proclaimed that asking people to say "cheese" was demeaning. He'd taken some excellent shots, some of which had been framed and put up around the school. They'd asked him to take the annual photo shoots, but he'd shrugged it off. He even said he didn't want his visual signature to be of people's faces, or something pompous to that effect.

The role of class photographer had gone to another local, Kev Pickering, or Mr. P as we called him.

Ryan had shown me what he meant one evening. He'd created a tiny dark room at home to try to teach himself photo development and he wanted me to see the difference between landscapes and people. Just as anyone who's passionate about something is, he wanted me to catch his vision. He'd explained to me that landscapes, even though they don't move, offer far more variety to his eye than people.

He showed me how the light and exposure could alter a scene. To prove his point, he also showed me three pictures he'd taken of people in his class. They all had the same glazed expression; you could almost see them disengaging as he took the pictures. I realised then that those people were reacting to him. They could see he himself had disengaged and they mirrored that behaviour back at him. Conversely, his passion for the wild gave him unique angles and interpretations of nature which translated to superb photography. Nature mirrored his passion back to him.

This remembered insight allowed me to guess that someone else had taken the pictures of Pete and the women, but also that it was the same person every time, the same person because they'd been able to elicit an animated response from the subject.

Pete had never had a consistent companion, though. It didn't make sense that he had a regular partner, anyway, with his lifestyle. Even if he had, they would almost certainly have baulked at taking endless pictures of him with beautiful young women who were clearly enamoured with him. I even tried examining the pictures with a magnifying glass to see if I could catch a glimpse of them in the sunglasses or a distant window. No such luck. That, too, demonstrated a slight photography skill that some people overlooked.

Find the photographer and you'll get to the truth, I said to myself.

Part of the problem with getting any more evidence was that it existed either within Harry's impenetrable codes or in other countries. I couldn't exactly just buy a Eurail Pass and hope to uncover the stories behind missing women who'd been gone for years. The photos I had from Pete had been coming since around the time the band had split up in 1980. Harry had had the right idea - centralising information and databases to get to the stuff that mattered.

The photos had been developed; digital photography was a recent development, so experienced photographers preferred to use the tools with which they were familiar. There weren't any clues about the kind of camera used, and I imagined that this would have changed over time.

It felt appropriate to update Cotton, even if his reaction was going to be volatile and unpredictable.

He lived in three or four different places, one of which was a country house on a large estate. It wasn't a mansion or a manor, by any standards, but it had expansive grounds and a small studio which he either used himself or allowed other musicians to take over when he wasn't around. This carefree attitude had given some new bands the chance to record demo albums for next to nothing, so he was seen as something of a patron of the arts. The house even came with its own recording label for bands who wanted to sign up: BHR - Ball House Records.

Besides the studio, the house also had separate apartments on the property. Cotton had told me that he preferred to stay in one of those, adding a layer of confusion to his personal security, but I'd been fairly certain this big secret was known to his friends and other hangers on.

I'd not had much luck with getting hold of him on the phone, so I drove up to his place. It was a twenty-minute drive from the nearest city, and the poplar trees and rhododendron hedges gave it plenty of security. The gate was open, so I got to drive all the way up to the front of the house. An older woman opened the door, let me in. I think she was a staff member. I noted the phones that were dotted around the house and wondered why no one answered them, but I guessed he'd asked everyone to leave them alone if they rang.

A man in his twenties with leather trousers and a vest showed me the way to Cotton's cottage apartment. I heard him before I saw him.

"Just get me on, man, I need this gig!" He was shouting into a phone, presumably one with a number I didn't know.

"If I can do one gig and save one person, that'd be pretty cool, doncha think? No, I don't need to get paid, that's not how this works. Just let me tell my story". He saw me looking at him through the open door, gesturing with his hand for me to wait.

"You're a saint! Heaven's missing an angel, dude, thank you!" He hung up the receiver with a flourish.

It was painful to hear him speaking like that, but he'd always seemed too lazy to use regular words and sentences. He just aimed for something that sounded more or less right and threw it out there.

"Finn! My man!"

I was back in his world.

After the initial shock I realised that he was a lot calmer than I'd seen him before. Still half-mad, but not as volatile. He told me that he'd been trying to do some charity work now that he was sober, so he could pay his dues and maybe get some kids to stay away from drugs. He'd had to make three attempts at rehab during his last efforts at sobriety before the final one took and he'd been on the straight and narrow ever since. I guessed that he was finding it hard to get guest spots on TV or radio because of his reputation and he agreed.

"A lifetime of screwing up - it gives other people certain expectations - and I probably deserve that. But I gotta keep trying. If I can get sober, anyone can."

I looked around his apartment. It was a mess, but there weren't bottles or bongs among the detritus.

"Proud of you, man, well done", I said, meaning it. "I wanted to fill you in on what's been going on. I gave him the full rundown, including the possibility that Pete could be some kind of intercontinental maniac.

He was horrified. He hadn't been following the news since he'd been sober, he found it magnified his paranoia. Like Leila, he was angry with himself for not realising something was off a lot earlier. He'd vouched for Pete in the industry, getting him onto hundreds of albums as a session musician. On many record sleeves, he was listed alongside big-name artists. Above all, he was disgusted that someone we knew could be involved in the vilest crimes imaginable.

You and me both, Cotton, you and me both.

He was slightly ameliorated by the news that Kaja had been identified, mostly due to his efforts and the financial backing that had gone into investigating the roots of her DNA.

"Man, the Lady in the Lake. Kaja. We should write a new song".

I suppose that's how he took things on board, translating them into his professional persona, but I wasn't willing to be a part of that.

"But now this thing with Pete, along with whatever the hell happened to Emery. No good, man, no good. How did we manage to spend so much time with him and not see it?". I could almost hear his thought processes at work, his mental gears trying to sync with the way all the stories came together in a confusing, awful climax. But then we both knew that it wasn't over yet, and it wouldn't be until Pete was arrested.

"Cotton, do you remember anyone who took photographs of Impressions, back in the day?" I was hoping he'd remember someone with a camera.

"You crazy? I can barely remember those years at all, never mind who was taking pictures. It felt like everyone was, everywhere we went. Snap! Snap! Snap! I think my eyesight is still suffering".

It was worth a try.

"Hang on, there was that one girlfriend of Pete's. She went everywhere with a camera".

I had no idea who he meant.

"Amelia. That's it. From Lakeside, too. Wow, I can't believe I remembered that!". He reached out to hi-five me, but I was trying to get my head around what he'd said.

Pete's girlfriend? Amelia had been my girlfriend. I wasn't jealous, since it had been decades ago, but I was certain that I'd been with her. I remembered she'd had that mild encounter with him that had ended quite quickly, so it was odd that Cotton had picked up on her time with Pete rather than me.

"Yeah, even when we were kids, she'd always be snapping away. Wasn't her old man a photographer?"

Pickering. Mr. P. The quiet, but friendly man who'd take the annual class photos. I'd forgotten it was Amelia's father.

"Yes! That's right, Cotton. Good memory, there - you see, you haven't fried your entire brain".

"Reason I remember is that she was also trying to find out about the Lady in the Lake. She kept on asking me if I would go down to the lake so she could take pictures of me there, but… nope… it was a big nope."

Again, I was struck by the way memory is like a spaghetti junction. I'd missed entire details of this case, details that other people had kept in the backs of their minds all along. Who would have thought that Cotton, who'd spent half his life abusing his brain cells, would have more intact memories than I had about certain aspects of our past.

I was glad for it, though, if only to recall just how close we'd all been.

"You know, at one stage, I thought she wanted to join our crew, or gang, whatever we were. I think Pete refused to let her in, though, he didn't want her to change the vibe we had."

That was weird. She'd not mentioned that to me, even when we hooked up for a time. Pete had never said a word about it, either.

Cotton was more focused than I'd seen him before.

"Clearing my head these past few weeks… months, it's been like lifting the mist. I'm remembering whole days from the past as if I was watching a TV programme. I can recall what people were wearing at specific moments. Like you, for example, Finn. You spent an entire year alternating the same two t-shirts. You had that one with the talking skull on it and the other was a picture of Elvis holding a gun. The same boots, every day. I'd say it was 1979."

He was right, although how he'd remembered that, I had no idea. I suddenly remembered the daily ritual of washing one and taking the other off the washing line. The skull was actually laughing into a speech bubble, but he was pretty close.

"But it's more than that. I remember how Pete kept on about how he'd met someone in a local town. He asked me to keep quiet about it, but the reason I remember it is that he was normally so aloof, distant about his love life."

I was taken aback that Cotton was stringing together sentences that didn't use made-up words or end in his version of a punchline. He gave people the impression that he took nothing seriously, since his default response to anything from good to bad news was a joke.

"I remember seeing Harry one day at the pub. He was just sitting, staring into space. No drink in front of him. He looked lost, and I had to say hello three times before he looked up. I'd never really looked at him before, he was always just there, but that day, I saw him differently. It was as though he was looking into the future or something."

"The worst part, though", he carried on, "is the influx of these memories about myself. It's like astral travel, man: I'll be watching a young Cotton doing stupid shit and there's nothing I can do about it. It haunts me. The good thing about the programme is that I get to share these memories with other people in recovery, and we've all got mad tales to tell".

I felt sorry for him. We'd always accepted his chaos as part of his nature, it never occurred to me that he could be at war with himself and what we were seeing were the manifestations of those battles. As kids, few were introspective to that degree; we all just lived life on a superficial level, echoing the live-fast-die-young bravado that was repeated to us by others in the music industry. Some of them actually fulfilled that statement, which is part of the reason I left the madness behind. I could see Cotton was only now having a chance to process it.

He wasn't stopping: "You know about amends, yeah? What I'm feeling right now is more than that. I need to make amends to myself for being such an idiot, but I've also had to cut off relationships and stop some of the, uh, business deals I was doing".

I think he meant drugs.

"Cotton, mate, I think I get it and I'm glad you're working through everything. There will be stuff you can't fix, though".

"Right, but I'll still do what I can." He ran a finger from teh crook of his elbow down his forearm. "I've got scars that aren't going to go away, but I can help other people stay away from getting scars".

I realised that all the trauma I'd been through, right from the discovery of the body in the lake to recent events was nothing compared with his own, self-created bombsite.

"Well, I'm glad you're healing, just take it… one day at a time, isn't that how they put it?"

"One hundred percent, pal. I'll do whatever you need me to do with this Pete business, just keep me in the loop. Kaja. Man. What a trip".

He handed me a card with his direct number on it and

we hugged. The remnants of our childhood friendship group, irrevocably damaged.

CHAPTER TWENTY-FOUR

Just let us do our jobs

Once again, I had to go to Leila to relate what Cotton had said. She listened intently, made a few notes and kept the friendly chatter to a minimum. It felt like I was in a relationship with two women, she was so good at dividing one aspect of her life from the other.

It wasn't really a surprise when, a few days later. Amelia turned up in town. She was staying at the Primrose Inn, since there weren't any other options. I saw her from a distance but she didn't see me.

Leila shut me off completely; she was in investigator mode, trying to piece together a complex case that needed her full focus. I wasn't going to be precious about being kept out of the loop, although my name was probably featured in a lot of the evidence documents. I knew that I wasn't a killer and that anywhere my name turned up in relation to these deaths it would be in a secondary, passive role.

A few days later, Leila filled me in.

She'd called Amelia and asked her to come to the UK for

further discussions. Not as an official person of interest and especially not as a suspect, just as a friend who may have some insights to offer. Leila could be caring and persuasive.

In a stunning turn of events, Amelia opened up a floodgate of information that appalled everyone, but also one that made complete sense.

The timeline I was given, second-hand, unfortunately, hinted at a trail of evidence that went right back to that spring of '75, to the time we discovered Kaja's body in the lake.

It was curious to hear the story from another person's point of view, once again, focusing on details I couldn't have known. Details that helped to fill in many gaps in my own story.

Amelia had been a loner. She'd loved photography and had admired my brother's work from afar. She'd been too shy to ask him for advice, but her father had given her the basics: a decent camera with a couple of lenses and some tips about lighting, exposure and focus. She said she had watched us boys as we rode around town but had also stayed back. As part of a project she created, she was taking pictures of us. She'd called it "Village Life", and wanted to project what it was like being a teen in a small village.

This had her trailing behind us on her own bike, sometimes on foot. She'd climb trees or hide behind buildings and bushes to get the right shots. They had to be candid, not posed.

I remembered what Ryan had said about disliking the artificial nature of portrait photography.

That spring, the one where everything happened, she'd been following us around, but Pete had gone to work and the rest of us had gone our separate ways. She'd lost track of Pete in his van heading towards the coast and had gone back to the lake to take some more pictures as the sun set on the water.

That's when everything changed for her, for Pete and for us.

She'd seen Pete arrive with his van at the lake after the sun had gone down. There was still some light. He'd unloaded something out of his van and into a boat. As he pulled away from the beach, she took a quick picture, and he'd turned around as the flash reflected off the water. He didn't seem to have seen her, so she packed up and left.

It was two days later that she realised what she'd probably seen, when the town fell into an uproar after we discovered the body. Terrified, she tried to stay inside and avoid speaking to anyone, but Pete had managed to find her. He'd climbed through a window at the back of her house while her father was out and just walked casually into her bedroom as if he'd been invited.

This is where her story differed from what she told us in Barcelona, a ruse that she'd made up on the spot to try and steer the focus onto him. She confessed that he'd threatened her. They'd not been in a relationship at all, he'd sat her down and explained what would happen to her if she ever talked. He did it with a half smile on his face that belied his threats.

She'd tried to put it behind her, making a show of trying to investigate the mysterious death of the Lady in the Lake, but not recording any evidence. Her notebook was full of doodles and random words she'd written down. After a time, the mood calmed down and the case cooled off. She made an effort to be as normal as possible, doing typical teenage things like going to the pubs, watching live bands. That's when she'd met up with me and we had our fling.

She'd admitted to Leila that the guilt of it all was killing her inside and that as much as she liked me, she'd realised that village life was just no place to exist with a monstrous secret. That was when she'd opted to leave the country.

When Leila had told me this, I'd been immensely sad for Amelia. I wasn't angry at her for lying, I was horrified that she'd had to go through this and that she hadn't been able to share it with me. One awful night had led to her having to leave the village forever.

Her narrative had continued: she had travelled in many different countries across Europe, enjoying her freedom and taking endless pictures of her surroundings. That experience had lasted for several months until one morning, she'd been on a promenade in the Côte d'Azur, taking in the fragrances and colours of the French Riviera when she'd felt someone take her elbow. It was Pete. He'd been charming and friendly, not a hint of a threat, and had been with a young woman who couldn't take her eyes off him. He'd introduced Amelia as a famous photographer friend and had begged her to take a picture of him and his girlfriend. She'd framed the shot, capturing the way the light sparkled in the woman's eyes and Pete's impenetrable gaze behind his mirrored shades. Shortly after that, they'd parted ways and Amelia had immediately made her way to another country, rattled.

After a couple of weeks in Rome, she'd made her way down to the gorgeous Amalfi coast and booked a room on Capri. Incredible views, faultless coastline panoramas. Then, late one afternoon, almost at sunset, a tug at her elbow. It was Pete, once again. The conversation was almost identical to the one they'd shared before as he introduced her to the woman he was with. That woman was eerily similar to the one in France: gorgeous, young, dark hair and a visible crush on Pete.

She'd taken the picture, as requested, and fled the country.

This time, she found herself in Barcelona, the larger city providing more of an escape and some chance at anonymity. It had taken a few months, but she'd set up a photography studio and had started to accrue clients.

It was at this point she'd admitted that there had never been a restaurant and that Tomás was also another twist to her story that she'd invented.

Once established, she felt that she'd finally escaped Pete and his international efforts at stalking her. But then he'd turned up at her studio with another woman by his side, requesting nothing more than a portrait. This happened a few more times. She'd have to travel across town to one of the beaches to take pictures of Pete and the women he was with. They'd all been similar in appearance and he maintained the same expression, that of a happy, wealthy and charismatic man on holiday.

Amelia had hated this intrusive behaviour but didn't have any energy left to try and avoid him. He never threatened her verbally, but his repeated presence itself was a threat. It said, *'it doesn't matter where you flee to, I will always find you and make sure that you are keeping your promise'*.

Years went by. When she tried to go on holiday, he'd turn up with his once-off girlfriends wherever she'd decided to visit. Eventually, she had a small stack of photos, almost identical, that she kept aside and didn't look at.

She said she'd sent those to me every now and then. He hadn't even had copies of those pictures, so she'd tried various tricks to keep her own identity a secret, putting down Pete's name along with hotel addresses on the backs of envelopes and then posting them from different cities around Europe.

She also admitted the truth about the thong and shells that he'd given her. It was the closest he'd come to admitting that he'd killed Kaja. He'd hissed into her ear one day that there were plenty of lakes around the area where she'd been visiting, but they were more dangerous than they appeared.

When things showed no sign of slowing down, and our story - the cold case and the recent body in the cellar - had appeared on her local news channel, she'd decided to try and send us hints, clues that wouldn't be linked back to her at all.

That's all she had to share.

Leila had to arrange for protection for Amelia and had removed her from the inn, taking her to a farmhouse somewhere. That's all I was allowed to know.

It made sense that she wasn't directly involved in the cases of missing women, especially Kaja's case, even if what she'd done could possibly be called withholding evidence. Besides, there was barely a trail connecting Pete to any kind of crimes, he'd been so effective at covering his tracks.

It was clear that the only person who'd be able to reveal the full story was on the run, somewhere on a boat in the Mediterranean. Being cautious, he was probably aware that his name was turning up in investigations, despite removing Harry from the search. It sounded like he was the person most likely responsible for Harry's death, given the close proximity Harry had reached in identifying Pete as a killer.

The word went out internationally from the cybercop teams, advising policing organisations to mobilise whatever resources they have and to dredge bodies of water situated close to holiday hotspots. The missing persons cases had something in common: women who had gone missing in holiday destinations outside of their own countries. Several Italian women who went missing in various Mediterranean countries. Some French nationals who vanished in Spain, Portugal and Malta. There wasn't a comprehensive list, but there were at least fifty missing persons who matched the profile. Only three had been positively linked to the pictures I'd given the unit. I'd given them twenty-five pictures in total.

The magnitude of the investigation was mind-boggling, and, despite efforts at keeping information to a minimum, the many countries and people involved resulted in details being leaked to the press.

Peter Fryer was Europe's Most Wanted.

CHAPTER TWENTY-FIVE

Origin Story

Shared histories, it seemed, were never shared. In the same way that everyone has their own tastes at a buffet table, individuals pick and choose the memories and experiences they recall from their childhood.

Lucien claimed that he couldn't remember much that had happened before the age of ten, saying that he always felt like an middle-aged man. I wanted to call his parents to ask them what they had to say about his formative years, but I had no idea who they were or even if they were still alive. It *was* hard to picture what he could have been like as a child. I imagined he frowned a lot.

Other people can recall with razor-sharp detail exact memories. For me, my early memories appear to have been quite selective, choosing the better ones to stay with me and leaving the rest behind.

After all, you can't remember every day of your childhood in linear form. Even if you had kept a diary every day, you'd still miss out on much of it. Also, you'd only be recording your perspective. With all the recent drama and given Cotton's transformation and subsequent recollection of the past, I wondered if I could dredge up ancient history. It seemed prudent to try; maybe there were clues from way back when we were small that would hint at future events.

I'd always thought that this horror had begun the day we found the Lady in the Lake - Kaja - when we were about fifteen, except for Pete, who was a little over sixteen. With Amelia's revelation that we hadn't discovered the body at all, since it was likely placed there by Pete, it meant that the origins of the nightmare started long before that day.

I pushed myself, trying to get as far back as I could, to where memories began.

Like most kids, your earliest memories are heavily reliant on family photographs. Those pictures often capture you as a baby, long before your mind was processing anything beyond eating and sleeping. The photographic record may include pics of you growing up, starting to walk, first day at school, blowing out candles on cakes at birthday parties and events like family Christmases. They're a great starting point - a prompt - for memories, but they're not the same as having actual memories.

Some adults go through hypnotherapy to try and make sense of childhood memories, being encouraged to regress on a journey through potential trauma so that the adult can heal. I wasn't sure I wanted to try that.

I'd spoken to Cotton, Ryan and Aiden. Emery and Harry were gone. Pete wasn't an option and Amelia was in hiding.

I called my parents. They were pleased to hear from me and asked me to come and join them for a weekend. I was certain that they'd have more information for me about what life was like in Lakeside in the 60s and early 70s. About the people who lived there and how they all related to each other.

It wasn't a long trip to the coast, I enjoyed the blue skies and the undulating fields next to the road. The countryside in that part of the world remained undeveloped with the housing projects or shopping malls that seemed to be consuming what little was left of the unspoiled scenery.

Mum and dad lived in a cul-de-sac in a retirement complex on the outskirts of their coastal town. It was a self-contained cottage that gave them the freedom they preferred but in sensible proximity to healthcare and 24-hour nursing, just in case.

There was a spare room that wasn't used much - I got the impression my brothers, just like me, weren't visiting enough.

They weren't *old*-old, they were just looking to make sure that their retirement was all arranged and that they wouldn't be a bother to anyone, in the no-fuss way that people of their generation had. I parked in their driveway and looked at the floral vines they'd grown on trellises on either side of the door. It was pretty. Mum opened up the door before I'd had a chance to ring the bell and I could smell freshly baked scones. There's something to be said for this experience, if you're lucky enough to have it; being able to return to your parents as an adult and to be treated like a beloved guest. It might make you regress a little, returning to childhood patterns of thinking and speech, but it can be therapeutic, too.

"Finlay!"

Hearing my full name was a good start. Nobody did that anymore. I made a mental note to introduce myself as Finlay more often. It gave me gravitas that the contraction didn't.

"Mum, thanks for having me! I mean, to visit, not as in giving birth". I figured a joke always helps break through any awkwardness.

She smiled and shook her head at the same time. My father was sitting in the lounge, watching a cricket match. He turned the sound down when I entered the room but left the TV on. Things had changed since I'd been a kid and television was only allowed in specific increments. Never when visitors were around.

We spent the afternoon catching up, they wanted to know how the shop was doing and I'd had to give a short version of the archaeology dig in the basement story.

From there, though, it was easier to start talking about

what had happened when I was 15, and then to reel them back even further. I asked them what Lakeside was like for them and how we'd got on as young kids there. They were quite happy to take a trip down memory lane, and I listened as they shared stories and corrected each other gently when one of them misremembered something.

Mum spoke of the ways she'd got to know other mothers back then and how she'd joined the church with that in mind. Back then it had been a large part of village life, so she made sure we went every week, even if it created an annoyance for her having to get three boys ready and then keep them in check during the service. She spoke about how some families were easier to get to know than others, that she'd made friends with Emery and Harry's parents, but that Pete's mother didn't go to church, so she was a bit of an enigma to her neighbours. She remembered Mr. Pickering, a "lovely man", by all accounts, and his attractive daughter. She recalled which couples had been married and mentioned a few names I wasn't aware of, people who had moved away from the village over the years.

Dad had added that he knew a few of the men from the pub, that they'd been, on the whole, uncomplicated husbands and fathers, just looking to make enough money to get by and have a nice time, maybe an annual holiday to the seaside. He brought up something I'd never known.

"I remember Fryer. Young Pete's dad."

That was interesting, since none of us had ever heard a single word about the man. It barely seemed possible that he even *had* a father.

"Jerry Fryer. He was older than most of the young dads by about ten years. It was a long time ago, but from what I remember, he'd been in the Second World War. It was like a part of him never came home, though. He killed himself just after Pete was born, and the police found a stash of old weapons in his basement. He was called Jerry Fryer because he'd been known for blowing up Germans. Sad, really, and we all felt for the mother, but she kept to herself. Best we could do was help them out by making sure young Pete could work before it was strictly legal at Benny's: the grocers".

I wasn't sure what to make of that. Losing a parent to suicide was unthinkable to me, and I'm sure that growing up, Pete must have struggled with that knowledge, too, even if his mother had only given him a sanitised version of the truth.

"The rest of you were just a bunch of tearaways. We didn't have a lot of rules for you, we just wanted you all to make sure you were back home for tea, and you didn't cause trouble for anyone else. You thought you could fool us with your hand-rolled cigarettes and the booze you drank at the village fetes, but we knew everything.

"We knew William was a bit of a head case, right from the start. He didn't have any boundaries, that one, just sang to his own tune."

William? Oh. *William*. Or Cotton, as we'd always known him. That amused me for some reason. He could have been Billy Ball. Or Willy. I was surprised the papers had never dug up his birth name. Maybe one day, I'd do that, just for a laugh.

My parents carried on speaking, as if the floodgates had been opened. They spoke about Aiden and Ryan and how they'd done so well for themselves, but that the bookshop had been the right thing for me, too. I wasn't sure if that meant they thought I had limited capacity for anything meaningful, but they weren't mean people, so I accepted it at face value. *"Ordinary Man Does Nothing in Particular"* - not exactly the headline the newspapers were looking for.

They spoke fondly of their time there, having lived in the village for almost thirty years, and, as they talked of the milder experiences they'd enjoyed, the gentle people they'd known and, in the ways of parents everywhere, of less complicated times, I was glad that they had these happy memories.

I wouldn't have minded some *less complicated times* of my own, but that wasn't on the cards any time soon.

It was a good weekend, though. I left feeling a bit lighter on my feet, hearing my father turn up the sound on the cricket as I closed the door. I hadn't given them a full rundown on what had been happening - that felt like it would have set them to worrying, although I'd let them know that I was seeing Leila and mum asked me to bring her round sometime soon.

Back in Blacksea I was struggling to settle back into a routine. As time passed, I wondered if Pete's boat had sunk, perhaps. He'd managed to vanish. He could be caught up in the seaweed at the bottom of the ocean, laughing forever as his hands waved with every shift of the currents.

As it turned out, I was very wrong on that count. He wasn't anywhere near the sea, he was on dry land and heading closer towards us every day.

CHAPTER TWENTY-SIX

All the wrong places

More bodies had turned up in the search relating to Harry's data. The current count was at nine, although it had proven difficult to say with any confidence that they all related to the same case. Some were several years old. They were remains, rather than bodies, in some cases, just bags of bones with some hair, clothing fragments and weights that had kept them out of sight.

Five of them had had shells stashed in their pockets or just rattling loose in the bags in which they'd been sent into the water.

It angered me that so many women could be regarded with such contempt by society, that they could vanish and not have the world turned on its head as friends and relatives looked for them, but I also knew that science had its limitations and that people make choices that don't make sense, too. A young woman might meet a man and be seduced into thinking that he is the one, abandoning common sense until it's too late and he has a hold on her, or, quite literally, has her in a chokehold. They may willingly walk away from families and jobs in search of true love and romance.

The women Amelia had spoken of all seemed to be happy and infatuated with Pete. They'd travelled from their home countries on holiday, maybe looking for a brief romance or something more sustainable and had seen something in Pete that told them he would meet those needs. His Gregory Peck looks and charm. With a tilt of his hat (had that really been all it took?) he'd transferred them into his scheme, taking ownership of their lives. I wondered if he knew that we knew and, if he did, what that would do to him. I doubted that he'd be overcome with remorse; it didn't seem possible that someone could commit such awful acts and retain a semblance of humanity. He was more predator than human, with the lethal, prowling aspect of a shark or a crocodile on the hunt, searching for weak spots to exploit. He was more likely to show pride, a sickening glow of proprietorship over what he'd done as if it displayed his superiority.

The international teams had created flyers with all the potential victims' faces on them. Seeing these women together was jarring. They were so similar, they looked like relatives. Dark hair, either parted or flowing loose. They had wide smiles and big eyes. So many that it looked like a full-page spread in a yearbook. I hadn't asked to see the remains that had been recovered, it beggared belief that so much life could be reduced to a small bag of bones.

I remembered how much my life had been affected by the discovery of Kaja and how many days I'd spent wondering who she was. I imagined these girls' parents and hoped that they were still alive so that they could get closure of some sort. How terrible to go to your grave never knowing the truth. In those countries, were there other men like me who'd grown up haunted by a time of confusion and loss emanating from their childhood?

The cybercrime team was contacted by numerous people with leads, people who claimed to know the identity of the dead women or said that they knew Pete's whereabouts. Those leads were mostly useless. A call came through from one person, though, who claimed to be on the flyer. She said that she had encountered Pete while hitching through Spain, but he'd given her a bad vibe. She used the same words that Amelia had, to describe the way that Pete had seemed… off.

On the day he'd invited her to enjoy him on a day trip into the mountains, she'd just left the country. The feeling he'd given her was so unsettling that she'd worked under an assumed name. Eventually, the assumed identity became her actual identity, so her missing persons case had never been resolved.

She had offered a full description of how he'd met her. He was sitting in the hotel foyer when she walked in to get the keys to her room. He had been reading a newspaper and then bumped into her as she was moving toward the hotel lift. In the process of apologising, he introduced himself and she hadn't felt any reason to think that this encounter was anything but a clumsy meeting.

He'd offered to show her around and she'd felt special, having this good-looking man taking her to the best nightspots. It was the perfect holiday romance. A crack had appeared when he'd read the news, though, and he'd become enraged with some minor story, completely out of proportion to what the story represented.

This woman had rage as one of her red flags on a date, so she'd decided not to take the friendship beyond that day. She also mentioned something that sounded like a pattern to me: when she'd asked him what was wrong, he ignored her and shut the conversation down. She said it was like being ghosted in real life. That reminded me of the innkeeper's daughter. It was anti-social behaviour that made him sound like a petulant child.

That behaviour was off-putting, but she also said that there was something in his eyes. They just became emotionless, lost their spark. That was the real impetus for her bailing on any future opportunities to be with him. She'd even written a postcard to her sister in which she'd referred to "Mister Dead Eyes", but she'd forgotten to post it.

Her description of her encounter with Pete was chilling to hear, given that he'd probably put the same techniques to work with other women. He'd developed a script that triggered the desired response, an almost fool-proof method of getting women to do what he wanted, as long as he managed to keep the facade going. He'd manipulate them into providing the words he needed to hear, making them settle into a dynamic that he'd established.

It was hateful, cynical and abusive, a far cry from the Pete I'd known. It's said, with truth, that many men excuse poor behaviour among their male friends, accepting abusive attitudes, awful jokes and even violence without a second thought. I didn't think I was like that, though.

If Cotton made an out-of-taste joke, I'd have called him on it. He'd usually agree that he'd stepped over the line. He was a shambles, personally, but he'd never been violent to women and he'd always made sure to avoid the kinds of relationships that could come back to haunt him as a musician. In particular, he'd been known to ask his minders to remove underage girls from his presence without a second thought.

Harry and Emery weren't red flag men, either. They weren't likely to be abusive in the ways in which they treated women, so I'd never had to correct their behaviour. Harry was shy with everyone, women and men, and Emery was almost a caricature of a family man, at least back before he'd leaned into his cult attitudes.

Pete's attitude during the time that we'd been friends and then played together in the band had always been above reproach. He was a bit of a lothario, being quick to sleep with women if they were available, but he, too, followed Cotton by making sure that they were old enough. At the time I'd known him, that meant a miniscule difference of a couple of years, so he wasn't old enough to be their dad or anything creepy.

He'd been friendly, charming, reserved and polite. While I wasn't into the revolving door lifestyle of his bedroom, it was a personal choice he'd made that didn't seem to need a rebuke.

Without wanting to blame any victims, I'd seen how quickly women had succumbed to him.

In retrospect, he'd weaponised that charm, and I could see how easily that could happen.

There was that one instance where there was a rumour that he'd fathered a child, but he'd gone to visit that young mother and had returned to us saying that she'd changed her mind. It never occurred to any of us to follow up to see what had happened, the rumour just faded away. It wasn't clear if she'd changed her mind about Pete being the father or if she'd terminated the pregnancy.

Considering everything that had happened recently, I wondered whether it was worth trying to find the person who'd made that claim, but I had no details to go on. It's tricky to prove a rumour. The reality was that there were more serious accusations and allegations on the go and that the police would be the ones finding out which angles to investigate to create a watertight case.

The most recent sightings of Pete had been in France, but there was nothing of substance to verify those sightings: no photographs at all.

I had begun to get anxious, realising that he may be carrying on his offence of charm, adding still more women to his collection. It was horrific to think that after all we knew, he could be getting away with it, more than twenty years on from the Lady in the Lake.

***

The shop had been doing quite well recently. The few news reports that had leaked out meant that people were curious. They'd take a day trip out to Blacksea before heading to Lakeside, to absorb the environment where everything that was being described had started. I wasn't always referred to by name in those media stories, especially the more slanderous ones, I was usually called "the bookseller", so it was an easy jump to make that I was the person involved, although Lucien had been approached a few times. When that happened, he said he just tried to look as mad as possible and retreat under his collars and beret. We found it quite funny; a moment of levity in a serious matter. I was occasionally asked to sign some of the true crime books I sold, even though I wasn't the author and had nothing to do with the contents.

In tandem with the shop's success, the inn was doing a roaring trade. Despite its nasty-looking interior, people were fascinated that Pete had stayed here, as well as Emery and Harry. *"Homicide Hotel - Victims and Killer"* would have looked good in a headline. Louise, the innkeeper's daughter who'd had her own run-in with Pete managed to keep her secret, and daydreamed instead of a time when she could transform the place with her modern touch. We'd chat in the street sometimes, giggling at the tourists with their maps and giving them the wrong directions.

Blacksea could be pretty when everyone stocked their window boxes with flowers and the sun was shining, so even if the visitors didn't get to see anything even vaguely related to any crimes, they left feeling relaxed.

I felt some comfort in the fact that as long as the place had so many visitors, it was unlikely that Pete would attempt a return.

With the extra crowds, Leila had to spend more time keeping the roads clear, making sure that people who'd been drinking weren't going to drive and generally being a friendly town cop. She'd wave at me when she was on duty and that made me smile. Anyone that dismissed her as a tame copper would be sorely surprised if they tried anything. I was sure she could take down anyone before they even realised it.

There was a general feeling that we were living in limbo, though, that peace would not last. Lucien would have dark moods where he'd talk about the calm before the storm, but there was no evidence to indicate that trouble was on the way. Moods are strange - you could just as easily be in a great mood for no apparent reason, and yet people were faster to assume the worst out of life.

I wondered how Amelia was doing in her place of safety,

whether she was missing her home in Barcelona - of course she would be - there's no comparison between a slightly damp English town and a city where the breeze blowing off the Mediterranean brings in promises of adventure every morning. I hoped for her sake that she'd be able to head back that way soon, and that she'd be able to put years of fear and stress behind her.

It turned out, Lucien was right. The storm was on the way.

CHAPTER TWENTY-SEVEN

The Resurrection

I'd opened the shop that morning at 9am, not that there was a queue waiting to get in. I fed TS, since that's what he demanded, and went downstairs to read the paper. Lucien was watching the shop, but he was more likely sitting with his nose in a novel, seeing some fantasy kingdom overlord being gutted by a dragon.

The post arrived.

Lucien called me.

"Finn, I think you should let the police open that one". It was marked Barcelona, and it was definitely not Amelia's handwriting. I had no other reason to receive mail from Barcelona besides her and she was somewhere close by.

Despite Lucien's caution, I opened the envelope. After all, if I took it to the cops, I'd never get to see what was inside, and I wanted to know.

It was a photo. Of Harry, dead.

I'd not seen this photo, and, from the looks of things, it wasn't an official crime scene photo, there were no little markers around the body. It was just my friend at his desk, with his hands resting on a note. I could read my name upside down in the photo. Along with the names of my friends. A photo taken by someone who had been right there, before the death was discovered.

That's all that was in the envelope. There were no other notes or clues.

After my hesitancy, I'd have to take it up to the police station after all. I grabbed my coat.

Leila's behaviour was unusual. I'd knocked on her office door and she'd jumped in her seat as if I'd given her a fright. She was normally calm, the kind of reassuring confidence you'd want around you in a crisis. Maybe the case is wearing her out, I thought to myself, but I pressed ahead with the news about the photograph. She barely seemed to hear.

"Finn, we need to talk. Off the record." I can't imagine too many people enjoying the phrase 'need to talk', record or not.

"What's up, Leila?"

"Let's go and have coffee".

We drove to a nearby village that was almost identical to Lakeside, only it wasn't next to a lake. There was a pretty cafe there, so it seemed like a decent option, even if we weren't there for cake, we were there 'to talk'.

She was shaking so much that her teacup rattled on the saucer as she drank it. Not a good sign. I hid my nerves behind my coffee mug, terrified that she was about to drop the 'let's be friends' line. At the same time, I couldn't recall any specific argument, disagreement or action that would have prompted that, so it was difficult to preempt a response to what I expected her to say. Turns out, I didn't need to.

"It's Emery". She exhaled as if she'd been underwater.

"Yes? He's been resurrected by his cult, has he?"

"In a manner of speaking, that's exactly right".

She'd lost me. I'd been expecting her to break up with me, not tell me that a man had risen from the dead.

"He was never dead - well, maybe for a few minutes - and he's currently alive and fully recovered from the gas leak experience."

"How's that possible, how come nobody told us?" I was shaken. I began to see why her nerves had been rattled that morning. too.

"That's above my pay grade. But here's where you come in. They need him to talk about what he'd been doing before he opened up the gas, but he won't say a word. At first, they assumed there was some brain damage; after all, he had died before being resuscitated. It's been weeks now. Apparently, on the weekend, he finally said he'll cop to everything, but only to you, Finn. He'll only talk to you, first, before he speaks to anyone else."

Once again, I felt like I'd been inserted into something I didn't understand and didn't want to understand, either. As much as this news was shocking and intriguing, I felt revolted by what he'd tried to do; it made me sick to my stomach.

"Not my problem, Leila. I've got nothing to say to him. He's a sick individual, someone I'd considered a friend who gave me nothing but betrayal in return. His kids, his wife! They didn't deserve that!".

Leila looked uncomfortable, she was playing with the sugar spoon in the bowl, churning it over like the words she was struggling to compile as she spoke.

"Finn, just take yourself out of the equation for a minute. Emery could have information that opens the door to a whole wealth of financial abuse, emotional manipulation bordering on criminal behaviour and possibly even human trafficking. We won't know the extent of it until he talks."

"Where is he?"

"This is as much as I've been allowed to find out: he's being held under a different identity in prison, isolated from the general population and under some trumped up charges relating to tax evasion. He's not able to leave and hasn't got the usual privileges like access to phone calls. As a flight risk and a potential danger to others and himself, he's been kept off the grid and under surveillance in his cell. The only option for you would be to go and visit him".

I was angry. Angry at Emery for dragging me into this, angry at Leila for giving me no choice at all and angry at just being powerless to avoid horror after horror, from murders to whatever Emery was up to. It was insane. I was just a bookseller in a small country town, not a detective, not a criminal mastermind, not a government agent. I just wanted to talk nonsense about the latest thrillers or literary fiction to people like me who preferred their far-fetched stories between the covers of a book. I had to count to ten before replying, but I still spoke between clenched teeth.

"You can see why I'm upset, right? Anyone in this position would be. I'll do it, but only because his wife and kids didn't deserve to be put in that position."

Leila was dismayed; I could see that she was desperately uncomfortable.

I carried on: "Leila, I know you aren't personally behind all this, and I guess it is difficult because our professional and personal magnets are pushing and pulling at the same time." I took her hands in mine. "Let's get past this and back to some kind of normality, okay?"

She nodded. "I'll set it up".

The prison was in another county. I'd be allowed to spend the day with Emery as the regular rules didn't apply to his incarceration.

It was a fortress of high red brick walls and razor wire, grilled windows and endless access gates that greeted me. I'd had to leave any belongings at the desk and was escorted down a series of passages that all looked identical. His cell door was open and there were two chairs placed opposite each other. I looked up at the corner of the cell, there were two cameras, one facing the chairs, the other his cot.

On the occasions when I'd last seen him, he'd been clad almost entirely in grey - suit, shirt, striped tie. His prison outfit was weirdly similar, a grey sweatshirt and trousers. Even his socks were grey, He wasn't wearing shoes or slippers. His face was paler than I remembered, as if he hadn't seen the sun for a long time. His mouth smiled a little, but his eyes told a different story.

"My God, Finn. I can't believe you came".

"Emery." I was struggling to stay composed.

"You're the only one who'll get it, I think. Even if you don't, I had to try".

"Just tell me what's so important. Why you've dragged me into this".

He sighed. Rubbed his eyes with his fists. "Just let me speak for a bit, it's going to sound crazy."

"Everything sounds crazy right now. You're dead, you're alive. Nothing is the way it's supposed to be". I gestured at him to go on.

His account of everything was so insane that it could just about be true.

According to Emery, he'd been squirrelling away funds from his organisation for years, maintaining a series of offshore accounts. He admitted that this was scandalous but that he'd also rationalised to himself that it was just business, that he deserved the recompense for his top-level input. He'd started avoiding the other leaders in the organisation, though, since they'd been having meetings that hinted at criminal activities on a larger scale.

Emery's own theft of funds was not what they were doing - he guessed that there was money laundering taking place and that some of the senior leaders were using the platform to move huge quantities of cash around the globe for secretive bodies, possibly Eastern European mob organisations. He wasn't sure, because he'd withdrawn at that point to protect himself and his family from them.

In an unrelated event that happened while we had rekindled our friendship during the body in the cellar case, Pete had come to visit him at home, asking a whole lot of questions about what he remembered from the Lady in the Lake events. They'd had coffee together, and he'd told Pete everything he knew, which was very little. The next thing he remembered was waking up in hospital, surrounded by people in suits and being questioned about a gas leak. They'd done toxicology reports on him and his family and found large traces of sedatives, but Emery had nothing to do with that.

After he'd recovered, he's been held in prison and subject to endless hours of questioning about why he'd tried to kill his family and what the extent of his involvement was in the organisation's criminal activities.

A few weeks later, a guard had mentioned to him that Pete was being investigated and was on the run, and he'd had the awful realisation that Pete wasn't just an old friend, but that he'd tried to take out him and his family in a fake murder-suicide event. It had enraged him, too, that Pete had treated his children as disposable.

The more he'd tried to piece it together, it seemed like the most obvious answer. No one in his organisation knew about his offshore accounts and it was Pete who had been there the day that they'd nearly died. Emery was horrified.

"We weren't some apocalyptic group looking to accelerate the end of the world by killing ourselves! I loved being alive. I loved my wife and kids!" He was weeping, shaking his head.

"There's no way I'd harm another person, I couldn't do that. That day is a blur, too, and there are gaps in my memory that I can't seem to fill. We didn't deserve to get treated like dogs being put down, and I'm stuck here in hell. My family is gone, and they want me to spill the beans on an organisation that would kill me if I ratted them out".

He was in a predicament, that's for sure.

I guess his story sounded plausible. To him, it was a mad connection to make that it could have been Pete who'd tried to kill him, since he had no idea the extent of the possible trail of slaughter and cover ups that Pete had been involved in. To me, though, it was quite possible that Pete had been willing to tidy up any connections to his past.

That last thought frightened me. It meant that I'd be on

his list, too, as would Cotton.

"I don't know what to say, Emery. I think you're right: Pete did try to take you off the table. As far as your organisation goes, I think you're stuck. Maybe they can give you some kind of immunity, witness protection?"

He looked devastated. "I have to disappear. Forever. I may as well have died".

"You'll be okay, you're protected in here and they want the guys at the top. As for Pete, the net is closing in. He can't get to you, and we'll make sure he's brought to book."

I filled him in on the full extent of Pete's nightmarish exploits as well as the identity of the Lady in the Lake.

"Finn, thank you. I'm so glad that someone believes me".

"We go back a long way, Emery. I've never been wild about your organisation, but we were kids together and I think we both want to rid ourselves of this lifelong hangover. It's difficult to say what happens next - I can't access the full scope of the investigations - but I think there's only one solution. Pete has to go down for what he's done, and he will".

"I guess the only route for me is to tell them what I know. It can't get worse than this; maybe they'll even let me see my family again. It kills me that they don't know what's happening and that they may think I tried to harm them. Who does that? Who hurts innocent people?"

We spent some more time talking about things that had nothing to do with murders, bodies, gas leaks or missing people. By the time I left, Emery had some colour in his cheeks and a slight spark of life had returned to his eyes. I pitied him, he would have a hard time trying to convince anyone of the truth, that Pete had staged the whole murder-suicide event and vanished.

"Till we meet again, Finn". He sounded like that was going to be unlikely.

After my initial reluctance to visit Emery, the trip home felt much more relaxed. I was relieved. He wasn't a deranged cult leader after all. He hadn't tried to kill his family. He'd even tried to do the right thing by shrinking back from whatever the other leaders in the organisation were doing.

People can be full of surprises. Cotton, sober and almost sane. Harry, a genius whose brilliance had reached out from beyond the grave and Emery, just a regular white-collar criminal whose greed had gotten the better of him.

I turned the spotlight on myself: as I looked at my part in all of this, I wasn't disappointed. I'd tried to find out the truth, even if the truth was always just out of reach. Despite the past lingering, I'd created a life I was proud of, a life that I hoped would return to some semblance of normalcy in the future. I'm sure Amelia, Emery, Leila and everyone else wanted the same thing for their own lives.

CHAPTER TWENTY-EIGHT

Knock, Knock. Who's there?

The Emery saga placed even more weight behind the theory that Pete had killed Harry. It may not have been his modus operandi, given that he seemed to prefer strangling women, but Harry wasn't his typical victim. On a level, he must have intuited that Harry was doing some intense investigation that could lead to the truth and opted to kill him rather than be exposed.

I wondered what Harry had thought in those final moments. Vindication? Terror? He seems to have figured out the broader details of the case, even if some of the evidence was missing. He'd not thought to protect himself, though. In the same situation, none of us would have believed that Pete, whom we'd known since he was a gangly child, would be a threat to us. Even now, as I considered that Pete could be after me, actively looking to remove any damning testimony I might have, I still recalled him as a friend, an ally.

It reminded me of Ted Bundy. During his trial he managed to entertain and manipulate people with his extreme charm. They seemed to forget for a moment the brutal charges he'd been attempting to defend himself against. His psychopathic behaviour wasn't evident in the courtroom, apart from his ability to deny any culpability and his belief in his own omnipotence - that he could game the system into seeing things his way.

From that perspective, I supposed I was a victim of Pete's manipulations. We all were. We saw what he chose to reveal to us. This control didn't just stop at his criminal behaviour, when I tried to see evidence of it from all our interactions it became quite apparent in the context of music.

The bass player has an unusual power in a rock band. In many setups, the bass player is the one who drives the energy of songs, asserting the link between the rhythm of percussion and the melody of guitars and keyboards. To the audience, the showmanship of the lead singer and lead guitarist may overshadow the contribution of the bass player, but the bass player may actually turn out to be the primary arranger of the songs, making sure they are cohesive and played according to their directives.

Cotton would have agreed: he just wanted the background music to keep going so that he could dominate the stage element, performing to the crowds and their expectations. Harry, too, was happy to keep the beat. Emery worked out melodies that fed into the lyrics, while I was happy to come up with catchy guitar riffs and rhythms that echoed the bass.

Thinking about the band reminded me, I needed to let Cotton know about Emery. I gave him a call on his top-secret number.

He was conflicted about the news; on the one hand, glad that Emery wasn't a complete nutter and that he was alive, but also concerned that Pete was a threat. He meant well and offered whatever resources we might need to catch Pete, but he wasn't prepared to get involved in the detective work.

He said he'd keep an eye out for anything unusual and ask his people not to let anyone onto the property.

That evening, I spent some time playing guitar, running through a few old songs and trying to recall some I'd forgotten. I'd played the instrument enough and practiced songs repeatedly till the day came that my fingers found their own way to the chords. It becomes easier over time. The moment my fingers curled around the fretboard, even years later, they formed the well-worn paths I'd learned so long ago.

I felt the neck of the guitar, smooth against my palm and looked at the battle scars across the body. I'd had a few instruments in my time, but this was my favourite one. The strings seemed to sing on their own, as if they were the ones creating the music and I was just doing what they told me to do. Leila was with me, watching quietly, half reading her book. She hadn't known me when I was in a band, and I didn't play much for fun anymore. I fell into a pattern of chords, picking out a note or two, and she began humming. She murmured a few words as lyrics, and somehow, we created a song, a beautiful moment that was not recorded and one that wouldn't be repeated; just emotions that slid out into the dark skies through the open window.

When you're a professional musician, it becomes tedious trying to come up with hit records. It removes the emotive sensuality that originally inspired you. The studio becomes a factory floor where everyone is churning away at their machines, trying to hit production targets. On stage, the performance either manifests as a natural moment of magic or, if the mood is off, an artificial attempt at creating something that's not there. It's unpredictable and frustrating: how can five people harness something so evanescent? I was in awe of musicians who were able to keep going, year after year, never losing their freshness or that sense of vulnerability. And I understood those musicians who pack it in rather than continue some thankless treadmill.

I'd given up on wanting to lead that lifestyle, but I still loved music when the mood struck me.

I thought about Pete. If, as the evidence suggested, he'd been on this murderous cycle for decades, how had he kept the dark desires going? Did he not tire of repeating the same cycle of seduction and destruction? It was unfathomable that he could satisfy those urges; it underscored the amount of control he must possess to do what he did and to make sure that it didn't escalate. He needed to be meticulous in his planning and execution, always finding the sick enthusiasm to carry on.

But then I'd never understood his capacity for sexual fulfilment. He was able to maintain that factory conveyor belt of women without getting bored. I'd seen that in action when we toured as a band, although he was only sleeping with them. I doubted that he was killing them back then but realised that he may also have been honing his skills with that, too, while we were distracted with setting up for gigs and having fun on the road. Perhaps, the music for him was secondary to the access he'd have to a constant stream of young women who were blinded to his faults, women who'd go willingly with him without coercion. It was possible that he gained no enjoyment from the sexual activities, but he'd been participating in them so that he could further use sex as a weapon, sex as a means of controlling his victims, who'd never suspect someone who was so physically present of having an agenda of violence and hatred.

If he'd been responsible for Kaja's death (and I was pretty certain that he was), his cravings must have started back when we were just kids, when the rest of us were happy to get a new pair of shoes or to have a few coins to buy chocolate.

Could it be related to his dead father, the craving? He'd not known the man and his mother hadn't shared too much about his father, either, as far as we knew. The village had taken a pact of silence on the way he'd died, opting instead to look after this child and his mum, left behind. But kids have questions. If he'd managed to find out the truth, that his father had been driven half-mad by what he'd done in the war, it may have fed into Pete's own psyche, causing him to question what he was capable of. Some theories exist that support generational madness, but I felt that was too close to the concept of the 'sins of the fathers', a shallow attempt at blaming evil on another generation.

I was no psychologist. Some days I barely knew what was

going on inside my own head, never mind someone else's.

Emery and Amelia were in hiding (with official help). Cotton was safe, too, staying put for now. That left me.

I had options, I could disappear for a while, go to my parents or another place altogether. Wait it out in the hopes that Pete would turn up and be arrested. I'd read a few True Crime books in my time, however, and I knew that people who wanted to stay hidden sometimes managed to do so. It was getting trickier to do that these days with international databases being shared, but it wasn't impossible. You could vanish into the vast Spanish countryside or become an anonymous low-level worker being paid off the books on an island that was virtually off the grid. There were cases where wanted people turned up after decades in foreign countries, sometimes even having wives and children; entire existences.

My hope was that this town and the village next to it would be safe, since both were central to Pete's story. If he was looking to evade capture, this would be the last place he'd come looking. He could send all the postcards, notes, photographs or even shells that he wanted via mail, I was off limits.

It never occurred to me that he may have been working with an accomplice. He'd tried to make Amelia his companion in guilt, but that had been an act of intimidation, of power. I suspected that his crimes were something he alone wanted to own, that his pride wouldn't allow him to work with anyone. The extent of his reign of terror, too, would have made it difficult for two people to be involved without that leading to complications of its own. There could only be one suspect.

The incident with Emery had been a good distraction, allowing police to head down a rabbit hole of investigation, as had Harry's murder. Brutal, cynical distractions that bought Pete time to plan for his next steps.

My next steps included getting a cup of coffee and chatting to some book suppliers to make sure that we had some good titles coming in.

A few weeks after my meeting with Emery, I happened to

be reading the local newspaper. It was strictly a community rag, in which businesses advertised and the journalists struggled to find anything of importance to place on the front page. It was probably one journalist and editor, the same person writing the stories and then editing them himself. There was a small item on page six that caught my eye: Mrs. Elsbeth Fryer had died. The obituary was short, referring to her as a long-standing resident of Lakeside. It mentioned neither her deceased husband nor her missing son. Pete was finally orphaned. The newspaper, not being discreet in any way at all, also advertised what looked like Pete's childhood home on their property page. It figured that the place would be empty, now. It was being described as the perfect second home for a country getaway or a quiet place ideal for retirement.

One by one, the houses in the village where I'd grown up were taking on new owners and identities. What if another skinny boy and his mother moved in. Would the child stare out of his bedroom window and covet the same freedoms that Pete had?

An adult with few responsibilities and a steady income has access to any number of opportunities to bring their unfulfilled childhood dreams to life. With the money I'd earned from the band, besides putting a substantial amount into the bookshop, I had bought a few things. One of them was a bicycle that was probably way too sophisticated for me. It was a light mountain bike that handled hills and bad roads like a dream, only I rarely used it.

I decided to take the bike over the hills to Lakeside, maybe have a spin around the village for old times' sake. I even packed a picnic like I was a kid, and this was an adventure.

It took me about an hour, red-faced and struggling, despite the expensive gears, to navigate the roads there. I'd never bought the lycra gear to go with the bike.

It offered a different point of view, drifting down the road into the village rather than driving in a car, and I enjoyed seeing the way woods and trees gave way to fields and the streams in the distance. Buzzing insects and drunken butterflies accompanied me. In the village, I saw a couple of people, but I didn't know them. I saw the For Sale sign outside Pete's house. The curtains were drawn. It was quiet, and even the pubs only had a couple of cars outside. The tourists had grown tired of making the trip here some time ago, almost as soon as the headlines died down.

It was mid-afternoon when I made it down to the lake. One of the boats wasn't chained to the others, so, on a whim, I climbed in and rowed out onto the cool water. This felt like where it had all started. There was no sense of dread, just a gentle circuit of the lake, gazing at the pier and two kids who were fishing on the opposite side. Perhaps knowing who Kaja was had brought some closure after all. I ate my picnic as the boat settled into the ripples created every time I moved.

After a time, I rowed back to the beach, hauled the boat up next to the others and sat down. It was utterly peaceful.

A shadow fell across me. It was some kind of intuition that let me know what was happening even before it took place.

"Hello, Pete," I said.

"Finn."

I didn't even turn around. I heard him move across the pebbles.

"We should talk", he said, using almost the same words that Leila had, only this time, a different kind of fear crept through my veins like ice water.

"You shouldn't be here, Pete. You should leave".

"Ah, Finn, you know this is where I belong. Part of me never left here, anyway".

I stood up. He was facing away from me, but his silhouette with the afternoon sun in front of him was unmistakable: long legs, tailored coat and a hat sitting at an angle that seemed to defy gravity.

"Let's talk then. Say what you need to say."

"The van". He gestured towards the car park where a white van was parked.

I followed him like an idiot child who has forgotten what his mother said about getting into cars with strangers. He picked up my bike and placed it in the van. Opened the passenger side door for me. If this was an abduction, it was the politest kidnapping ever to have taken place. I swung myself into the seat and closed the door.

He started the engine and turned away from the lake. I watched in the side mirror as it faded into the background of reeds, trees and then hills.

Pete seemed at ease as he drove, occasionally turning to me and smiling. It was as though we were on a road trip, heading out on holiday. "Let's stop here", he said. We sat at the top of a hill overlooking a wide valley. I could see some farmhouses and another village to my left, but we were far away from people.

"1975". He shook his head. "I was 16, thought I was grown up, for sure. I'd hang out with the men at the pubs, drinking beer but not enjoying it, I just wanted to be there, to fit in. I was doing deliveries, riding all over, seeing every inch of this county. One evening, I got a bit drunk. This bloke offered me a ride. I agreed - didn't want to mess up my work van.

"He rode around for ages. Then he sees this hitchhiker. She was wearing one of those kaftans, all loose hair and smiles. She had a strange accent, and I could smell the sweat on her as she sat between us, like she hadn't had a bath for a day or two. This man, he takes us up here to this hilltop, this layby. Parks his red van and says to us we should get out, enjoy the view. We did. I think the girl was a bit stoned; she kept on giggling and touching his chest. I was still buzzing from the beer.

"Then things changed, he started trying to kiss her. She's turning her face, this way and that, not playing along at all. He looks me in the eye as if to say 'watch this' and he just starts throttling her with his bare hands. He's still watching me, I'm frozen in place, and I can see he's getting excited, it's bringing him some perverse pleasure. She's swatting at him with her hands until they drop to her sides and her head tilts backwards. She's gone.

"He tells me to help him as he picks her up and we swing her body into the bracken. I can see she's pissed herself and I can smell it on my hands. I haven't said anything for ages. We get back into his van, roar off down the hill and he drops me off back at the pub. Doesn't say a word, just grins and drives off."

Pete has been looking up at the sky while talking, as if he's addressing the moon.

"The next night, I drove back up there in my own van. She was still there. I picked her up and put her in the back. She looked quite calm. I had a few shell trinkets that I'd picked up at an archaeological dig when I delivered vegetables to their tents one day. I took one and put it around her neck to cover up the bruising. I drove back down to the lake and rowed out there, almost where you were today, put her body in the reeds. Her kaftan was gone, I had no idea where it was. She was naked.

"I couldn't stop thinking about her, how beautiful she was and how quietly she'd died, as if accepting her fate. It moved me. I'd always thought death was violent and ugly and had never realised there could be poetry and music in it.

I was listening to him, getting increasingly anxious at his reveries.

"I took you all there the next day so you could also share in her beauty, but it broke the spell. You all panicked, didn't see it the way I'd wanted you to see it.

"Just before we went to the lake, I saw that same man, in his red van. Fresh Lamb. He was just driving out of town. I never saw him again."

Pete looked away. His shoulders sagged in a way that I'd never seen before on him: defeated.

"It was like I'd always been asleep before that day, but watching that girl die, it felt like her life was transferred into me, I felt her joy for a moment. My sadness lifted and I felt no remorse about her death. That man gave me a wonderful gift, he opened my eyes to this world of pleasure where death can bring the ultimate rush."

Completely fucking mad. That was what I was thinking as

he shared his memories of that time, a period of horror for the rest of us. I'd always thought Cotton was the crazy one, not this calm, self-assured psycho that was sitting beside me, describing murder as if he was Wordsworth reciting Daffodils for the first time.

I spoke for the first time in ages.

"Her name was Kaja Trojak. She was seventeen. She loved her parents back in Poland and came here to find a life. That was taken from here before she'd even finished her childhood. Why did you not just go to the police, why did you keep silent and let us struggle to find answers?"

I was trying to understand myself, why I wasn't attempting to push him to the ground, fight him, scream at him.

He laughed.

"I'd just found out what it was to be born again. I wanted more than anything to experience that again and again. It became my life's goal to be there, helping women to experience the joy of giving someone the most perfect gift, the ultimate surrender.

"The sensation died down after a while, and I thought to myself, where can someone like me, trapped in a little village, find more carefree women looking to experience life to the fullest. That's when I suggested we start a band. I knew all about the lifestyle musicians got to enjoy and I wanted that, and more".

The band had been invented so that Pete Fryer could have access to young women to murder. My brain could hardly cope with that information.

"And it worked! We got to tour, play concerts, travel to the continent and meet so many beautiful creatures! When Cotton left, I just carried on in the background, staying in the industry but keeping a low profile and then using every opportunity to travel to the kinds of places where there would be single women with dreams of romance in their hearts. It felt like the more intoxicated they were with their own dreams, the more powerful the translation made at the point when they left this world."

He stood up, dusted off his trousers.

"You can't imagine how much perfection I've seen in this life. I found out what Harry was doing because he admitted as much before he knew he was actually tracking me. He was boasting that he was close to getting to the bottom of the Lady in the Lake. He had to go. I took little pleasure in that".

"Amelia?" I said.

"She was always around with her camera, and I thought it could be the perfect way of capturing the joy of my experiences on film. You'll see the bliss in their faces. Amelia couldn't say no, she was terrified. Quite rightly so, I saw the flash of her camera that night. When she didn't talk to the police about it, I knew I could count on her to keep her mouth shut, I just had to give her a reminder of that every now and then. I was fond of her, too, but she was too frightened of this world for me to help transition, she needed to stay here and find joy her own way".

"How many? How many, Pete?"

"Not all of them. Some were just little fish that I cast back into their stupid ponds. Only the special ones got to share that ultimate moment of beauty with me".

I didn't know what to say. He noticed.

"I do things on my own terms, Finn. Always have. Always will."

At that, he gestured for me to follow him, so I got back into the van. He drove all the way back into Blacksea, right up to the front door of the shop. This deranged man had brought me home.

I got my bike out of the back of the van and tried to think of something to say. Nothing came to mind - what *could* you say to this litany of madness - and he waved and drove away.

CHAPTER TWENTY-NINE

Second Impressions

Lucien took one look at my face and knew something was dreadfully wrong.

"You look sick, mate, you okay?"

I confirmed his diagnosis by running to the toilet and vomiting repeatedly.

Leila dropped everything, literally running down the road to meet me when I called her. Momentarily, she dropped her fierce DI persona and took me in her arms, kissed my face all over as if to confirm that I was still there, alive.

It felt like I'd been a part of a nightmare - Pete's passion-filled confession that bordered on an outpouring of lust seemed unreal, like I'd had a fever dream. She calmed me down, comforted me and let me absorb the horror before taking me back to the police station where she assumed her role once again.

"He's back", she said.

"Yes, he's back, and he's quite mad. He doesn't seem to get the enormity of what he's done at all. There's no remorse. He admitted killing Harry and that it hadn't brought him the same amount of pleasure, but that was no admission of guilt, believe me."

As difficult as it was, I repeated what he'd said to me, with Leila recording my version of his confession. It reiterated most of what she'd suspected, only fleshing it out with a motive that made no sense. If *red-van-man* had never taken him on that trip, would he have just carried on with his ordinary life?

The news that he was back was complex. Leila knew that there was an international manhunt underway, but the activity around that had died down somewhat since he hadn't surfaced. The obvious choice would be to bring down the full weight of every law enforcement agency in the country, to shut down roads, search every inch of every field, village, hill and town. Corner him as if he was a fox slipping across familiar territory trying to avoid the hunt. It could have generated the kind of hysteria that would drive Pete into hiding, and it was all too apparent that he was excellent at vanishing when he chose to.

A preposterous idea occurred to me. The very kind of inspired, yet mad, genius plan that might just work.

I laid out my concept for Leila, who struggled not to let her emotions show on her face. I asked her to make a few calls to see if we could put the plan into motion.

Pete's psychopathy was rooted in experiences from his childhood. The band was born out of those experiences at the same time as his journey into being a full-blown serial killer came to pass. He'd created the band as a mechanism to support his madness.

I called Cotton. Once again, bearing awful news, but he seemed less strung out by it. He'd already taken measures to secure his estate, and despite what had happened with Harry, didn't seem to think Pete posed much of a threat to him.

"Cotton, this insanity has gone on for too long. I'm desperate to get back to the life I had before everything went south. How do you feel about playing a gig?"

He didn't say anything for a while. I wasn't sure if he was laughing or crying, he was making some strange sounds.

"A gig, Finn? We haven't played together in years. It's hard to play when you're riding the sober horse, man, she goes one way when the fans want you to go another way. They expect me to be on a wild ride, and she just trots quietly along".

"I get that, really, I do, but I think our friends deserve it. Think of it as a benefit gig. 'Friends with Benefits'." I thought he'd appreciate the stupid joke, but he was struggling to get his head around it.

I had a thought. "We do something small, set up a marquee tent at your place. I mean, you've got all that space, and you'd have more control over who comes in and out. You could invite everyone who's anyone in the industry".

"What? Next, you'll be having us doing a singalong like Do They Know It's Christmas. Nice idea, but it ain't really us."

I grinned at the idea of Sting, Boy George and Bono trying to stay cool in a tent in Cotton's garden while the cameras filmed us doing a song. *Lady in the Lake* was no pop anthem, even with the treatment that the other band had given it.

"I just think Harry deserves it. Okay, so you don't want to be in the limelight right now, we keep our names off the bill. We'd need a session drummer, a lead guitarist and a bass player, but I think we could get it going. One last time on stage for our childhood gang. We could call it Second Impressions."

Cotton was the kind of person who'd do things on a whim. He'd change his mind, do the unexpected. That frustrated the producers in the recording studio, since every take sounded different, but it made life interesting for everyone around him.

"Second thoughts," he said, "let's do it. I've got a few ideas that could work, and none of them involve Bob Geldof. Sure, we can donate the funds to charity, but we don't need to make a crude display of it."

I knew he was actually mates with Geldof, so I laughed.

He continued: "Maybe Ringo can fill in on drums and McCartney on bass?"

It was the sort of ridiculous exchange we both needed to take the edge off the mood.

"Leave it to me, Finlay Jones, leave it to me". He cut the call with a Mephistophelian chuckle.

And I did. He was a popular face in the music world, whereas I was a nobody. He'd lasted for so long when others faded out either dramatically or anonymously. Somehow, he survived a war that he'd inflicted on his own body, coming back from life-threatening injuries and overdoses time after time. And yet he retained a certain charisma since he was not the kind of person to harm others, he always tried to get on with people, not trying to steal their place in the spotlight. He'd never needed to.

What have I done, I thought, as I made my way downstairs to put in a bit of practice on my guitar.

Two days later, Leila arrived in the shop, looking like she was bursting with news that she wanted to share.

"Go on then", I said.

"It's a done deal. Emery will be able to join your gig, but only at the last minute. We'll have him brought to the concert and delivered to the stage. He'll be disguised for his own protection, and you can't expose his identity. But he'll be there".

Amazing. I couldn't believe she'd managed to pull it off. "I guess we'll have to go big or go home, hey?"

She nodded. "It's going to be wild. I think Harry would have loved it".

Harry had never been particularly ebullient, but I think she was right. He would have enjoyed this mad experience. It suited the atmosphere we'd created as a band back in the late 70s, a wild ride of entertainment with a few unexpected twists at every gig.

There wouldn't be time to rehearse with Emery, but I was sure that he'd be fine. He'd always managed to produce note-perfect renditions of songs - it was probably his classical training that gave him the edge, allowing him to become part of the music in the same way that Harry seemed to achieve his flow with numbers and codes.

Ah, Harry. I remembered his quietness. His round face and

wide eyes that didn't express rage, it just welcomed whatever was on the table, going along with the mood and not entering into conflicts. In the hierarchy of a band, drummers are often the ones to come and go. Maybe they joined because they could play a bit and every band needs one, until they realised they didn't like the style of music, or they found the lead singer annoying. Some drummers took the party-hard lifestyle to heart and either became such hopeless junkies or drunks that they could no longer keep a beat, or their own hearts fell out of syncopation with their bodies. It was easier to replace a drummer than, say, a lead guitarist, without the fans complaining, it seemed. I saw Harry as a force of cohesion to the band - he'd brought an element of ordinariness that stabilised the range of personalities the rest of us represented.

Harry.

After another week, I packed up my guitar and some clothes and headed out to Cotton's estate. On the way I turned the car radio up way too loud to drown out any intrusive thoughts that might try and talk me out of what I was about to do. It was a road trip to the unknown and I couldn't turn back.

High security at Cotton's front gate was comforting. He'd made sure that this was an invitation-only affair and I had to show mine before being allowed access. There were trucks lining his driveway and people in work gear setting up a vast marquee in the distance. I'd not realised just how huge his garden was. His house may have been modest, even though it had a couple of guest cottages, but the land stretched out forever. I could see the sun setting over the hills and basked in its last-gasp warmth for a moment.

I saw Leila now and then over the next two days as they set up security for the event. She'd managed to rope in a full team and was walking around with an earpiece in like a Secret Service agent. It was sobering, a reminder that what we were doing wasn't just a party, it was in memory of someone we'd known all our lives, and that his killer could be anywhere.

The night before was the final rehearsal, we did our sound

checks, and the session players Cotton had roped in weren't bad at all. He'd even requested that his agent find three people to resemble Harry, Emery and Pete, so it felt like we were one of those bizarre tribute bands, The Impressions (of Impressions). It felt good to be on stage; far removed from the state of crisis I'd been operating under. Just getting lost in the chords, the rhythm and the tunes. Cotton wasn't quite as wild as I'd anticipated, but I assumed he was saving himself for the actual event. He was taking the soundcheck seriously, helping the extras to get the songs right.

That was our soundcheck, there were a few other big-name acts doing theirs, too, so being backstage was like browsing through a who's-who of music over the past two decades. The theme had been Second Impressions, giving many semi-retired players the chance to come out of the woodwork with no expectations that they'd need to churn out hit songs or go on the road again.

Older musicians can be quite amusing. Many had replaced their former hardcore lifestyles with regimens of sobriety, the manifestations of which included meditation, the presence of lifestyle coaches, bottled water and a strict ban on any substances in the dressing rooms, which were a few caravans down the hill from the marquee. It felt more like a wellness retreat than a concert.

Their roadies moved with intent, bulky, powerful men in cut-off t-shirts and heavy boots. There were more wives than groupies, too, an unusual take on the excesses of rock. While I had the right lanyard on, no one recognised me, so I was able to blend into the crowds with ease.

Ego is a powerful motivator. I'd seen that in the dispassionate way that Pete had narrated his story. What to anyone else would be a recitation of horror was simply about him being able to do exactly as he pleased without consequences. He was convinced that no one would ever be able to get in the way of what he was doing and that he could just take what he wanted, when he wanted it.

This was the purpose of the concert: to draw him out of hiding with the knowledge that his band was performing without him, that the glory no longer belonged to him. His session and touring musician career and all the perks of international travel that went with it were over. He wouldn't be able to get on anyone's private jet or yacht and be able to target women anymore. He'd be enraged that his omnipotence had flaws in it that could cause his orgy of self-indulgence to end. It was a guess, but we hoped it would be an informed one: he would come out of hiding and somehow try to access the event.

CHAPTER THIRTY

The Day the Music Burned

If anything, life had proven to me that it was unpredictable; I could never have foreseen how things would go down on the night of the Second Impressions concert.

It went well, to begin with. A decent crowd of people: industry people, friends and friends of friends. There was a happy mood. Performances are strange beasts. You can play to a crowd that's animated and excited one night and then the following night, for no reason at all, the mood is totally different: sulky, aggressive and difficult to turn. Fortunately, the novelty of this get-together had inspired people to put on their best faces.

A couple of bands did their warm-up shows - they'd also opted to make the evening a collaborative one, welcoming in guest stars to do unexpected duets. We were due to go on later in the evening, so I took a walk to calm myself a bit. I saw the security teams combing the perimeter in the distance with torches. There were spotlights, too, but I didn't see Leila. I imagined that she'd be in the control room with the Head of Security, maybe checking out the monitors to see that everything was covered.

It was time to head to the stage. Cotton was excitable. Sober, but still on a natural high and in his element. He was doing stretching exercises and doing little runs on the spot, loosening up for the stage posturing and dancing he'd be doing in a moment. I felt a tap on my shoulder. I turned around, nodded and then faced the front again. Did a double take. It was Emery. He was wearing a baseball cap and a black t-shirt with the word CREW on it, just like the teams who were setting up the equipment. He'd made it. Cotton was stunned, he'd not had the chance to process what had happened with Emery, so they caught up for a few minutes. Emery's replacement musician retired with good grace - he'd still be paid, and he was enjoying this musical smorgasbord. He'd probably get a chance to fill in with another band later on. A moment's silence. I could hear a continuity person introducing us.

Then, the spotlights.

We went straight into a couple of our most popular songs, and the crowd got into it. It was odd - we'd never been guaranteed hitmakers when we'd actually performed together in the late 70s, but our reputation had gained a bit of a cult following over the years, enhanced by the re-release of our music catalogue on CD. Cotton was quite emotional. He introduced the song that brought us all together by dedicating it by shouting 'this one's for Kaja': Lady in the Lake, and we went at it; Cotton, Emery and me all sharing the microphone, with the bass player going full guns and the drummer taking on a solo right in the middle that would have been Harry's. I guessed a few people may have been wondering about Emery's crew t-shirt, especially since he was supposed to be dead, but that was exactly the kind of impact we'd been hoping to create.

As the song ended, there was a commotion at the back of the marquee. It was hard to see with the lights in our faces, but I could tell people were running, scattering. Cotton called for everyone to be calm, a security person came up to the stage and asked Cotton to make an announcement. There had been a small fire, but it was contained, so we could carry on. We played our slot with as much energy as we'd had as kids, and each of us gave a short speech at the end, honouring Harry and thanking everyone for coming. We didn't mention Pete.

The evening continued in style, act after act taking the stage and performing each song as if it were their last.

Emery came to me outside the marquee.

"I've got to go, Finn". He didn't look sad, he looked like he'd been enjoying the party of a lifetime, which I suppose he had been.

"We'll get through this; we'll get you out, Emery". I was feeling quite emotional.

"Nah, you don't need to. I've got some time in prison coming to me anyway because of the money business". He meant tax evasion, but I understood.

"You'll be safer in there while Pete's out and about. Probably better for a while."

He nodded. "It was good to see you all again and to play together. I won't forget that".

He turned and blended in at once with the crew members who were criss-crossing the backstage area with various pieces of equipment.

I sat down on a speaker, suddenly feeling deflated. It had been the most incredible evening, but Pete had been a no-show, so the entire premise of it had failed. I was disappointed - we'd been so convinced that this would lure Pete out of hiding, but our trap hadn't worked. He was that jittery that he'd stayed put. I wondered if we'd ever see him again, or if this show would force him underground forever.

How was Leila going to justify this to her bosses? I made my way to the security caravan where the monitors displayed what was happening around the estate. As I got there, I could tell there was some rushed activity going on.

"Yeah, DI Stanbury - no one got eyes on her?" The security boss was speaking into his radio. "I need a full perimeter search, all teams".

He saw me waiting at the door.

"Where is she?" I asked.

"We don't know. There were some reports around the time of the fire that she'd been in some kind of altercation, so we're checking to see if she's alright. No one's seen her for a while; an earpiece was found; we think it's hers".

As he spoke, I didn't need a detective's badge to understand what had happened. It was exactly what we'd expected: Pete *had* turned up. He'd done exactly what his inner voice had told him to. Maybe Leila had spotted him, or he'd spotted her. Either way, it hadn't ended well. My stomach sank with disgust and fear.

"I think he's got her", I said, knowing even as I said it that I was right.

There was no way of closing down the event, it was just too vast and complex. If he'd managed to get in, he must have managed to get out again. While Harry had been excellent at blending into the background in situations, Pete had always had a knack for arriving and leaving as if he'd carried one of those magician's smoke balls in his pocket and he'd materialised straight into the room in his long coat and hat. You could be talking to him and suddenly you'd realise that he'd vanished.

I found Cotton in his caravan where he'd been cooling off and changing and told him what had probably happened. I shouldn't have done that. He was beside himself, blaming the entire thing on his own actions. He threw a bottle of water at the caravan window, smashing it.

"We messed up, Finn. We blew it".

"We haven't messed up; we knew he'd turn up here. We just need to figure out where he'd go from here". I knew, even as I said that, exactly where we'd find him. "You stay here. I've got to go", I told Cotton.

"You can't just leave, what if he's here, waiting to get all of us?"

"He's gone, and I can't waste any time sitting around to find out. Just keep this party going and make sure that tonight really does honour Harry".

He shrugged. "I've got it. Go, Finn, go!"

It was the longest drive of my life, through the moonlit fields and down country roads that didn't allow for speeding as they sometimes narrowed to a single lane. The side of the car was being whipped by vegetation that grew in the shade of trees set back from the road.

It had been reckless, I realised, trying to coax a serial killer out of hiding by baiting him. He'd always shown that he thinks ten steps ahead of everyone else, and the loopholes we'd left could prove fatal. He'd most likely have wanted to appear on stage with us and would have, had he not encountered Leila in the crowds. We'd also put all the other guests in danger by not giving them the full picture. He could have set the whole tent aflame, engulfing a vast chunk of the music industry in one go. It was bad enough that he'd seemingly slipped in and out; what he could have done was unthinkable.

I opened the window, letting the night breeze lash at my cheeks trying to clear my head as I drove, hoping to formulate a plan that wouldn't put Leila at any more risk. If it wasn't already too late, that is.

There were clouds on the hills as I screeched to a stop in the gravel in Lakeside. The moon still shone across the water of the lake, sending yellow streaks across the black water and the indigo shadows surrounding it.

In the middle of the lake, I could see a white shape, large and still.

There was a boat that was left at the edge of the water, the bottom of it damp, surrounded by footprints in the sand. I shoved it away from the edge, jumped in with my shoes soaking wet and steered to the centre of the lake, the centre of everything: this was where it all began.

As I got there, I could see it was human, and leaned over the edge of the boat to vomit. Still retching, the boat moving under the momentum of my frenzied rowing, I reached the person. She was floating on her back like that famous Pre-

Raphaelite painting of a drowned Ophelia, her hair twisting into the weeds, dress billowing. Her hands were raised upwards, fingers trailing in the water. Her face was oddly tranquil, as if she'd simply laid down to sleep.

Amelia.

Confusion passed over me, I had known that this place held some kind of evil attraction to Pete, that he was drawn to it, returning to the dark waters again and again, perhaps to relive that night of awakening.

This was where I'd been sure that I'd find him with Leila, yet instead, here was Amelia, lost and found. She'd been in a safe house, somewhere and hadn't been on my mind for the past few weeks with the concert arrangements. It seemed impossible that she, not Leila, lay here, her outstretched fingers causing gentle ripples on the surface of the lake.

I struggled to get her on board the boat, almost tipping over a few times, but eventually got her body into the craft. She was ice cold. I eased the boat back to shore, carried her up to the small hospital, even though I knew she was beyond help.

There was just one more place where I may find Pete, but I wasn't sure how to get there.

I had to sit in the car with my eyes closed for a bit, trying to let his words flow back into my memory: he'd described how that man in the red van had driven them all over the place before they'd picked up a hitchhiker, Kaja, and then they'd driven still more until they got to a… hilltop with a layby and the view of a valley below them.

It was difficult to imagine which hill it could be. If I picked the wrong one, I could be on the opposite side of that same valley.

On the way I passed through Blacksea and made a stop at the police station. I explained what had happened and that I needed help. Leila's colleagues were shocked, but they leapt into action. The officer on duty called others in and they arrived in their private vehicles, red-cheeked from the rush in waking up to getting dressed and coming in to work. There was a large map of the area in the back office and we quickly flagged each hilltop that was straddled by a road overlooking the valley.

The officer on duty tried to get me to stay in town but once I'd seen where everyone was going and made sure that each hill was covered, I pushed past him and ran to my car.

Once again, I struggled to keep the small vehicle on the road as I swerved through country lanes, hoping that no farmers would be pulling out of their gates and that no sheep would be wandering into the roadway. The highest point in the area was at the top of Giant's Pass, a vast green bulge that rose above all the other hills to offer a panoramic view of the area.

Grey stone walls flashed past, with cottages in the distance. Most were completely dark, only a couple had lights on. Clouds obscured the moon, but it was so bright that their silver linings reminded me of that day when I'd pictured the Fingers of God reaching down from sunlit skies to land on Amelia's face. She'd always seemed like a character from another era, a timeless princess who had merely stopped by on her travels through time to hold court wherever she ended up.

She was gone, now, this friend and lover, the woman whose ability to capture life through her lens had been captured in a final snapshot that I'd never be able to forget, a photograph taken by my mind's eye as she lay in all her perfection upon the surface of the lake.

I wished I'd kept her with me, all those years ago, that she'd stayed with me in Lakeside. Not as my wife, she was too elusive a beauty for that, but so that she could have stayed safe. I'd fallen in love again, with Leila, being one of those people for whom it's possible to know love twice in their lifetime, but now I faced the prospect of losing both in the space of just a few hours.

The top of the hill rolled into view, and I slowed down, turned off my headlights.

CHAPTER THIRTY-ONE

On a clear day, you can see forever

I could see a torchlight shining behind some ferns on the left-hand side of the road. It wasn't moving, it must have been propped up against a rock.

Like a statue positioned in a place of honour, I could see Pete's back, his long coat and hat in silhouette against the sky.

He turned towards me.

I stopped the car, tried to catch my breath, and walked towards him. He was just standing, admiring the view. A few feet away, I saw Leila. She was still, her form half covered in bracken, facing away from me. She wasn't wearing clothes, and her dark skin was barely visible in the shadows. I was too late.

Then, I saw her back move as she drew in a breath.

Pete spoke, his voice deep and rasping.

"You can't have an Impressions concert without all of us", he said.

"We can't have all of us, Pete. You murdered Harry".

"You always thought Cotton was the leader of the band. How naive of you. I made sure we worked together. I created us. I decided when it was over, and I should have been there tonight. You performed your little trick, resurrecting Emery, but we could have been so much bigger than that".

"Amelia didn't deserve what you did".

"Amelia was always just a nothing, a shadow of a person. She stole people's souls with her endless photographs. I gave her more than she could ever have wanted. In the end, without me, she went back to not existing at all."

"We were friends, Pete, all of us".

"Friendship is an illusion. Loneliness is reality; we're all alone, whether we are surrounded by crowds like Cotton or we're cowering in an apartment in Barcelona".

I tried to steer him towards saying anything that didn't sound delusional.

"Pete, maybe this goes back to what your father did so long ago. He was at war with himself, just like you are".

"He was weak. Pathetic. He'd only ever followed orders so when the orders stopped coming, he was lost. He didn't even have the strength to be a father. I *fathered* myself".

I could see headlights across the hills on every side of the valley, the bowl that stretched out below us. Police and others on the search for Leila. They spread out like veins.

"It's time to end this, Pete. You know it, I know it. The man in the red van is gone. Your father is gone. Harry is gone. Every single woman you coveted, and stole is gone. All you have left is the promise of prison".

"You think I haven't been in prison all my life? This world is a jail cell, a prison yard where you only get to do what you want for a few minutes every day, otherwise, you're working for someone else for their goals, for their dreams."

I saw Leila roll slightly, groaning. Pete looked at her.

"She was never part of this.", I said.

"Oh, I know that" he said, laughing, "the police are like so many ants, just following each other to a picnic and never looking at the feast that's everywhere around them. They are the embodiment of the meaningless rules we make up, slaves to imaginary legislation that is designed to dehumanise us. Women are just there to serve a purpose, whether that's serving men in power or just making sure that more people are born into slavery".

I thought of how his mother had worked so hard to keep their little family going when he was a child.

"I remember your mum. She worked two jobs for you, to give you the opportunities she thought you deserved. The last thing she knew of you was that you are the embodiment of evil, that you squandered it all and destroyed so many lives in the process".

"Oh, fuck off, you preachy little shit", he said.

I'd touched a nerve.

"No, you fuck off, you worthless… nobody". I'd tried to dig for the worst insult I could in the hopes of offending him.

"I'm the only *somebody*," he said, "you've got it all wrong. We're all lied to, told we can be whatever we want to be, but that's just not true. Most of us are nobodies; I'm here to help them see that".

He turned away to look at the view once again, as if looking out on the souls of the people he'd killed, lost in thought.

Behind my back, I'd been carrying a heavy, hardback book. It was an illustrated guide to bird life in the region, maybe 1,200 pages. A bookseller always has books.

I slammed it into his head, and he went down, flailing his arms as he tried to keep his balance. I stepped forward and hit him again as he tried to stand and he staggered towards a small outcrop of rocks down the slope. He slid away into the darkness, I could hear the crash of the bracken as he broke through it, and I caught glimpses of him as he broke through the bushes down the hill.

After a moment, the noise stopped, but I was sure he'd escaped; the book was a good deterrent, but it wasn't a lethal weapon.

Leila had rolled onto her back. She'd been wrapped in a scarf, but it didn't cover her breasts and I could see bruising and blood across her face and body. She looked like she had some burns, too. I wrapped her in my coat and helped her to my car. She was almost unconscious as I drove back down the hill towards town, groaning from the back seat where I'd let her lie.

My only aim was to get her to medical care; to save her from whatever injuries she'd picked up. She was alive.

At the hospital in Blacksea, she was taken from me on a gurney, still not fully conscious. I watched the orderlies wheel her away as the ER doctor tried to assess what was wrong with her.

In the lobby, I paced, not sure what to do next. It had been a night of adrenalin, aggression and violence, and I was unable to calm myself.

Twice I'd had to listen to him as he rambled on about himself. Twice I could have beaten him, attacked him, subdued him and yet he'd managed to get away. I was angry at myself and the tears just started coming, tears for Leila and her broken body. Tears for Amelia who'd gone to join Harry wherever dead people go. I'd not considered the full weight of religion since I'd been to church as a child. My experience of it had not been a spiritual one, it was more about good behaviour and people judging each other based on supposition and appearances. Despite myself, I prayed, slumped over in a salmon-coloured chair surrounded by nurses and families of patients. The clink of the vending machines that disgorged drinks and snacks was the only sound apart from my murmured supplication.

There was no point in staying at the hospital; I asked them to call me if Leila woke up, and they'd agreed with some reluctance.

Back home, I called Cotton.

The concert had ended but I could still hear music over the phone. It was the last of the partygoers. Night owls for whom life wasn't restricted to daylight.

He was glad that Leila was alive, appalled at the news that Amelia was dead and revolted by Pete, by what he'd said and done and the fact that he'd evaded capture once again. There wasn't much else to say. What *could* we say?

I assumed Emery was back in prison, safely behind bars. It wasn't possible for me to contact him, so I just made a note to get word to him as soon as I had the chance. It was almost morning, so I slept, a deep sleep without dreams.

It was hard to stay at home, where Leila and I had shared so many hours, wintering with our books and board games, sharing meals and laughter and the warmth of each other's bodies. The place was as silent as it had been that morning when I found that body in the basement, as quiet as the cemetery for one that it had once been. Lucien turned up later in the morning, reading as he walked, somehow managing to avoid bumping into door frames and bookshelves. He looked up, saw my face and realised that I wasn't in a good way. He made us some tea and we sat in silence for an hour.

Eventually, he spoke.

"Finn, mate, you've tried everything. Maybe it's time to let it go. Let the coppers do their work".

"I can't. Leila deserves better."

"I get it: you want to fix things, but you're not a detective. You're not a special agent. We've done what we can, but we're just booksellers."

"Everything I know is tied up in this. I won't get myself back until we've caught him".

"He doesn't care, Finn. He's only looking after number one, and he'll get rid of anyone in his way".

Lucien did have a point. We had no training, no resources and no agencies backing us up. All we had were ghosts. Kaja, Amelia, Harry and the host of women Pete had made disappear. He was a dangerous man. I was just a bookseller who might not have a large, heavy volume next time I saw him.

"Let me think. I need to think", I said. Lucien wandered off into the shop, straightening piles of books as he went.

The phone rang in the late afternoon. It was the hospital.

I headed back there, parked in the small parking lot and navigated my way to her ward. In the room, there were no bunches of flowers as I'd seen in other wards and I felt embarrassed for a second, as if I should have paused amid all the trauma to buy a bunch of flowers. The absurdity of grief.

Leila was propped up in bed. She was facing the window and had bandages across her face, a drip in her arm.

She turned slightly when she heard me in the room, and I went across to the side of her bed. She tried to smile, then tried to apologise, but her mouth was swollen and bruised.

"I should never have put you in that position, Leila".

She shook her head, managed to say, "Not your fault", but it came together as if it was one word; she was struggling to speak. Her eyes were struggling to focus. She closed them and went to sleep. I kissed her forehead.

The doctor didn't have much to say apart from the fact that she was alive, no lasting damage, but she'd been through an ordeal. They were monitoring her for any physical aftereffects and that it's possible she might display signs of PTSD. Shock can manifest in many forms, apparently.

I wondered what it must be like for regular people, people who didn't end up in newspaper headlines or tangled up in murders. If it was possible that an ordinary person could just grow up in a pleasant place, go to school, get a job, have a family and progress through an unruffled old age until, one day, they died peacefully in bed with their loved ones around them. The more I spoke to people, the less likely this scenario seemed. The more common one was of perfectly innocent families being interrupted by illness or accidents that seemed totally unjust. It wasn't just that bad things happened to good people, but that all people should anticipate an expectation of life that should be, as Hobbes suggested, "nasty, brutish and short. Hobbes wasn't feted for his views; others around him saw his outlook as pessimistic. He attempted to back it up by saying that without laws and a societal framework, people would resort to the most egregious criminal behaviour. As far as I could see, even with laws and a functioning society in place, terrible things happened.

I was determined that Leila's life and my own would not be nasty, brutish and short.

The brutality of it all made it hard to be optimistic. I was in a dark mood, and I realised that the only way to shake it off would be to reset my thinking, so I went out to the car, put on the radio and listened to music. It's hard to be angry when you hear the ways in which humans can turn notes into melodies and melodies into beauty.

I lost track of how long I sat there. People passing by must have thought I was mad, a lone lunatic sitting in his car with the volume up on his sound system, but no one knocked on my window and told me to stop.

Classical music, punk, grunge, rap, folk, rock, jazz, blues; it didn't matter what I was playing, it all spoke to me. The lyrics, the guitars, drums, flutes, keyboards, bass, trumpets. Each song was like diving into a pool of emotions to be refreshed and restored. It washed over me.

But then the whole artificial cathedral of happiness imploded. For some unknown reason, my own band's recording made its way into the speakers:

"She's a lady, make no mistake,
Where others bend she had to break,
In the reeds upon the lake.
Do you hear the wind in the trees,
Look there and you might see me,
Can you see she's swimming free,
The lady, the lady in the lake".

I thumped the dashboard with both fists, desperate to get the song out of my head. It wasn't just the song, it was the way it was made, in the aftermath of that destructive afternoon when we discovered Kaja's body. When I thought of that, I remembered the way Amelia had ended up in an almost identical spot. It enraged me.

The feelings that it stirred up were too complex to process, especially since this song had been quite unusual in the way we'd written it: each of us had contributed a line of the lyrics, and I remembered how strange that had been in the studio.

The memory caused me to pause. I pictured us, Cotton, Me, Emery, Pete and Harry.

It took a moment for the penny to drop. I'd never made the connection, even after Pete had admitted to leaving Kaja's body there, staging the position of it for us all to find.

Pete's line:

"Do you hear the wind in the trees,
Look there and you might see me".

Oh.

The rest of us were trying to articulate something we didn't understand. Pete understood completely. He'd been there all along. Without him, there would have been no Lady in the Lake.

I thought of the vast body of water that was the lake, its depths unfathomable due to its blackness. I knew that some lakes and lochs could be hundreds of metres deep, and ours was much shallower than that, but it felt like if you were to dive in you could just keep on going into the darkness forever. I thought of Loch Ness, which was just over two hundred metres deep and yet its depths were mysterious and impenetrable enough to allow for the legend of the Monster to exist.

Around our lake the woods that tracked the winding paths of the streams that led to it converged, fringing it on almost every side except for the stretch where the pebble beach and sandy shore was, where boats could be launched. If you were looking at the lake, you'd see the water. Maybe the reeds and a few birds that skimmed their way across it. You might not even notice the trees. Or anyone using the trees as cover.

What if Pete's couplet in that song wasn't just a poetic ad lib, but he meant for us to take it at face value. What if this had been his sly admittance that he was there all along?

CHAPTER THIRTY-TWO

The willows in the wind

Statistically, the more I headed out onto the lake in a small boat, the more likely I was going to encounter a dead person, given my past experiences. Instead, I decided to drive out to the other side by heading around that body of water. It would mean a substantial detour since the waterways that fed the lake only had a couple of areas with bridges, but it seemed more cautious to approach that way rather than from the surface of the lake, where I'd be entirely exposed to view, should anyone be watching.

On the way, I stopped at the shop. Called Lucien over and told him my theory. He had a vivid imagination and viewpoints that were often different to mine, so I valued what he had to say. Too often, I just did what I wanted to anyway, but he seemed to have great clarity in this current situation that I found baffling.

He tilted his head at me, processing what I'd said.

"So you think there is a homicidal maniac and he is in the woods", he said.

"That about sums it up", I said, looking at the mud on my Dr. Martens.

"And you think the best course of action is to go there, on your own".

"Well, yes."

"You like movies, right?"

I'd lost him; he was coming at me from left field, once again. "Sure, but this is real life?"

"In your typical horror movie, whether it's a teen slasher flick or a film noir drama, what should you *never* do if there's the possibility that a killer is hiding in the woods?

I was getting a bit annoyed with his tone. "Lucien, I'm not a co-ed exchange student, I think I can handle myself. I've been with him twice recently and he hasn't tried to hurt me".

"But you tried to brain him with a bird book".

Lucien had a point.

He looked me in the eye. "Mr. Jones, as your most valued employee, I would like to request that you ensure the longevity of my employment by not engaging in this action".

"As my *only* employee", I said, "I can let you know that I'll be happy for you to take it over if something happens to me."

"Finn, don't do it, man". He looked despondent.

"If I'm not back in a few hours, let the cops know where to look for me".

I was never a leader at school or after that. No one came to me for advice, I wasn't that kind of person. I wasn't an idiot, mind, but some people ooze confidence and opinions. They become CEOs and politicians, no matter how foolish their opinions turn out to be. I leaned more towards being a follower, as long as I trusted the leadership of those whom I was following. According to Pete, I'd been led by him all along, so not only was I not a leader, but I was also quite bad at choosing whom to follow, too.

Lucien said I should hold on. He went to get a notepad and made me write down what I'd said, about the bookshop going to him if something should happen to me and what I was planning on doing so he could tell the cops, as well as instructions to send them after me at a certain time.

It wasn't a legal document by any stretch of the imagination, but I signed it with flair, hoping to offer him some reassurance.

"And if Leila should phone - I doubt she will - maybe keep this to yourself. She's been through a lot".

That wasn't kind of me. I know that it's always better to show your cards, to tell the truth and not conceal things in a relationship, especially not a showdown with a maniac, but I felt responsible for putting her life at risk once, I wasn't going to do that a second time.

Lucien saw me to the door and watched as I headed for the car.

"Thanks for everything, Lucien, make sure the windows are closed when you leave".

"Good luck, boss", he said, dolefully.

This time, I had a walking stick with me. It wasn't meant to be used as a weapon, but it might help as some form of defence should I need to get away in a hurry. The roads were still quite empty as I headed through town, slowing down just enough to wave at the hospital.

"I'll be back, Leila, I promise". I hoped I wasn't lying.

It took about half an hour to cross the farmlands on old roads, including the two arched stone bridges along the way. The car was bumping along farm tracks after we left the tarred road, and I patted the dashboard protectively. "Keep going, car, just keep going".

As even the track started to become impassable, I started overthinking this excursion. *"Man Killed in Forest Fury"*, the headlines would read.

There was a turnstile at the edge of the woods that I'd not seen very often, I hadn't spent much time in the woods since I'd been a child, and not after the body was found in the lake. It took a while for anyone to get used to moving about the area without looking over their shoulder, since no one was ever caught for the killing.

I still knew my way around. There was a wide path that took you to a fork, and if you wanted to head down to the edge of the lake you had to take the right-hand path of the fork. Even if I had forgotten that the local walkers had installed marker posts with coloured notches on them, so you'd know which path to take. The woods weren't that expansive - I doubt anyone had ever been lost in them - but it's always safer to stick to the main path. My walking stick slashed at the weeds that grew in the mud, and I could see tracks where a horse and rider must have recently come. It wasn't much of a hike; you could bring your dogs here and let them run around and many people did.

As I started to second guess my pathfinding skills, I heard a rustle to my right, coming from inside a cluster of bushes. My nerves were on high alert, so I ducked, only to see the red flash of a fox as it darted away, belly held low to the ground and its tail saluting me.

The path curved to the left and then to the right as it crossed over a stream where a couple of boulders formed a natural bridge. In the distance, I could hear the sound of a swan; the water must be near. Finally, I saw gaps in the trees, the long, drooping fronds of the willows that flicked against the surface of the lake in a gentle breeze. The wind sliced through their lime-green blades, whistling and stirring. Weeping.

An entire continent was searching for Pete, and even our own county was on high alert for him. It scarcely seemed possible that he'd turn up in this place, just a couple of hundred metres from where he'd created the first part of his own awful legend.

"Pete!" I was sick of this charade. "It's over!"

I walked closer to the edge of the water. There was a bird hide set up on the bank above the reeds, almost invisible until you were upon it. That's how the local bird watchers preferred it, so they could spend time in the hut tracking different species drawn to the body of water across the seasons.

The ground was damp as I neared the building. I could

hear heavy breathing, like a wounded cow, coming from inside.

It was him.

He was half seated with his back propped up against the wooden wall. His hat was gone, and his coat was torn and filthy. He was holding his leg. I could see his trousers were split up to the knee and it looked like a broken bone was protruding from his calf. He must have smashed it on his way down the hill after I'd sent him half-falling onto the rocks.

He didn't say anything, just shook his head.

"I should just leave you to die here, but it's too pretty", I said, meaning every word. "You've destroyed so much in this life, it's time for it to end."

He looked at me, grinned weirdly. "Finn, Finn, Finn. They'll never take me alive. My dad may have been useless, but he did leave something behind for me".

He held up his hand in front of his face. He was holding an old, corroded hand grenade.

I put my hand out as if to stop him, backing up as I did so.

As I hit the frame of the hide with my shoulder, I saw him pull the pin, and ran and dove into the woods, falling against weeds and saplings, clutching at piles of damp and rotting leaves.

Nothing happened.

I rolled over, picking the vegetation off my face, surprised that I'd survived.

After a few minutes, when I could hear his laboured breathing again and my heart had stopped yammering in my chest, I made my way back to the hide. The hand grenade was lying on the ground. It hadn't gone off. Pete was beyond caring, clutching his leg and perspiring in agony.

I sat with him while we waited for the police. He kept watching me, unable to speak. He lay there like a giant beached trout, his mouth gasping and incapable of harming anyone else.

I had no sympathy for him. It wasn't enough suffering. The concept of an eternity in hell couldn't even hint at the injustice he'd caused and the punishment he deserved.

But I'm just an ordinary man, a bookseller and former musician, not a vigilante seeking revenge.

As far as I could see, any revenge story just sparked endless vendettas: eyes for eyes, teeth for teeth. I wanted no part of that. I wanted justice for my lost friends and for those parts of my childhood that he'd stolen, but even justice cannot account for those losses.

I heard footsteps coming. He was done.

CHAPTER THIRTY-THREE

All roads converge

I was helped to my feet by the police who waited for the paramedics to arrive. I was fine, physically, but couldn't shake the adrenalin that was still pumping through my veins. They kept me far away from Pete; I couldn't see what was going on, but I heard him call out in pain a few times.

The teams helped me back to my car and one of Leila's colleagues drove me back into town. He rode in silence, aware of the complex situation he was dealing with, an alleged killer, apprehended. His boss's partner on the scene. I suppose he didn't know what to say and wanted to avoid getting into any trouble. After he dropped me and the car at home, I watched as he strode back to the police station. He was probably composing the story he'd be telling for the rest of his career, positioning himself right in the thick of it.

The news was full of this story for weeks afterwards, so I kept the television off and stayed inside as much as possible.

Leila tried to keep me out of it as she dealt with all the reports that were needed to tie up the loose ends, but then, one morning, she called me up.

"You're not going to believe this".
But not much surprised me anymore.

They'd brought over Amelia's things from Barcelona. It had taken a while to get permission and for everything to arrive. In the process of cataloguing everything and in the hopes that she'd have kept more evidence, even more photos were found.

They were similar to the ones I'd received; pictures of me and my friends in the village, as she'd sought to capture our lives in film. She'd been exceptionally detailed, taking multiple angles of all the buildings, the people coming and going and the village as it appeared with different shades of green as the sun shone overhead or ducked behind clouds.

Among those pictures was something that caught Leila's eye. There, parked in front of the Town Hall. It was barely the right colour, having faded to burnt umber rather than red, but Amelia's eye for detail had captured it in detail, right down to the large sticker on the back: Fresh Lamb. You could even read the number plate. If Pete's story was to be believed, this was the exact van that had taken him along for a joy ride, stopping to pick up a young hitchhiker along the way.

The news distressed me; I'd been trying to create the illusion that it was all over and that we'd finally broken the spell. Leila reassured me that she'd follow up on it and that I could just let it go.

She did. A4 posters were put up everywhere in the district, stuck on lamp posts and in windows: *Do You Know This Van?*

It seemed like a long shot. Who could possibly remember a random vehicle from twenty years ago? In a quirk of fate, someone did.

She called the police station in a panic, asking if she had to come in. They told her that it would be best to talk to her in person. Stranger still, she wanted me to be there when she told them what she knew. I was starting to feel like I should have become a professional detective or investigator, since no matter what I tried to do to avoid getting involved, crime and its maelstrom of information seemed to pull me in.

I agreed to meet at the station, despite my reluctance.

Leila hadn't told me who the person was, hoping that the surprise would create an atmosphere more conducive to natural reactions from both of us. She was right - I was shocked.

Rosemary Coonan. The librarian.

Leila introduced us as if we'd never met, and, while I'd hoped to be seated at the back of the room, I was offered a seat at the metal desk opposite Rosemary. She didn't look at the detectives or at Leila, she looked at me.

"Finn, thank you for coming. I was scared and didn't know what to do. I don't have a lawyer or anything like that".

"Rosemary, don't worry, you can just tell them everything you know, I'm sure you'll be fine."

She was shaking a bit, and I could see tears welling up in her eyes.

"I recognised that van immediately. It was my brother's. Well, not his: more specifically, he was driving it for a while back then, doing deliveries, I suppose. He was on the road a lot in those days. I think he liked to drive most at night so he could clear his mind. He wasn't well."

If the person driving that van had been Pete's mentor, I had no doubt that he wasn't well.

"The thing is, he came through to Blacksea and popped in to visit me, offered me some pieces of lamb that he had left over after making his deliveries. I remember doubting how fresh it would be if he'd driven all that way, but he'd just laughed at me. We weren't that close, and he didn't stay long. Said he had places to be, people to see, or something. I haven't seen him since. Deliberately."

Her choice of words there seemed unlike her, she was usually not the kind of person who'd gossip or hold a grudge against someone.

"What he was doing, what he did; it's nothing I want to hear about, ever again. Those poor women. For the life of me, I don't know where he lost it."

Women. That sounded too familiar.

"They got him eventually, and the whole family was horrified. I'd moved here when I was young to get away from that family, they were vicious. My dad was violent, and my mum just took it. I chose the library to opt for the most peaceful space I could so I wouldn't have to be in their world at all".

"He's been in prison for so long now that sometimes I have the luxury of forgetting about him completely, it's a part of my life that I don't talk about. But then I see this van and the floodgates open up. Oh, how awful".

She went on to explain that her brother had been responsible for several murders in the 70s and that he'd been arrested, found guilty and sentenced to prison. While in prison, he changed his name to avoid being singled out by the other convicts, but he still managed to maintain a level of notoriety that was positively evil.

Rosemary had to whisper his name; the interview room fell silent for an entire minute.

She seemed broken by the time she'd finished telling her story, and I was miserable for her, knowing what it was like to have been, unwittingly, close to someone who turned out to be without the regular moral codes by which the rest of us lived. She chose the library; I had the bookshop. Those were inefficient shields against the traumas life had dealt us.

I reached across the table and took her hand. It was wet from the tears she'd been shedding the whole time. She didn't say anything after that, it was as though she'd given everything she had to give in that awful interview.

The man in the red van had been more of a father to Pete within a short encounter than Pete's own father had ever been, inspiring him to take a brutal and lifelong diversion from society. He'd handed him the keys to his own future and left with a slap of his hand against his door panel. I wondered if he'd known what he'd done, and the red van man had laughed when he'd heard about the body in the lake.

It was unthinkable that two killers had plied their trade in this insignificant corner of the world, and that they'd managed to get away with it for so long.

Kaja had never stood a chance.

The interview had concluded after that. Rosemary was thanked for being brave, but I could tell it would be some time before she would be up to facing life again.

Leila kept me informed afterwards, just the bare details, not the entire investigation. They'd tracked down her brother in prison and he hadn't admitted anything. He didn't admit to being in Blacksea or Lakeside. He ignored questions about the red van and delivering meat and seemed to be in conflict: on the one hand, wanting to hear all the details while on the other, distancing himself from them. He didn't confess to killing a beautiful, young Polish hitchhiker on a warm evening in spring, 1975 and he refused to even acknowledge his sister.

Amelia's ingenuity and fascination with photography and her eye for detail had reached out from beyond the grave to resolve the greatest mystery we'd known as children. Although Kaja's killer hadn't offered a full confession, all the details had come together to provide a snapshot of what had happened on that fateful day, when none of us had been adult enough to find answers and any semblance of our childhood had come to an abrupt end.

It had been as simple as tracking down the driver of a van that had happened to drive through the village one day, and yet it had propelled one of us on a murderous streak that almost went undiscovered, had it not been for her frightened, desperate attempts at bringing him to justice.

My own part in this was minimal, I'd been drawn in because of my proximity to everything and everyone, unable to extract myself from the pull of the whirlpool as it grew beyond our control.

CHAPTER THIRTY-FOUR

The quiet life

In the months that followed, life nudged its way back to normality. Leila moved in with me into our bookshop cottage, but she still kept her job up at the station. Her professional life settled down to a more pedestrian style of policing. She continued to track down the gang who'd been poaching, eventually managing to make arrests and seeing those through to convictions and prison sentences. She wasn't just a delightful companion; she was a force to be reckoned with when it came to the law.

We spent weekends at a place we bought at the beach and had enough money coming in from music royalties to buy a small boat that we'd take out to sea when the weather was calm. We called her *Amelia's Hope*.

Lucien was glad that we made it back, even if he had to quietly hide the "I'm the BOSS" mug he'd bought himself, just in case I hadn't returned. He was happy enough to potter around the shop, entertaining the few customers who came and went. The shop was never going to be a huge success, but as the local murders entered into legend, they gained folklore status, so we'd get some curious tourists popping by to see where it all happened. No one asked for my autograph.

Last I heard, Emery managed to cut a deal, offering up some information about the higher-ups in his organisation. Arrests were made, and, seeing as he was officially dead, he was able to make the transition to assuming a new life. I don't think he was able to reclaim his wife and children, but he'd made a life of positive thinking, so of all of us, he was best positioned to make the adjustment.

Cotton was doing well, but we'd agreed to put The Impressions to bed forever, so we just kept up with each other on the phone occasionally. Last I'd heard he'd bankrolled a website that hosted some musicians, he was hoping that the internet would be the next big thing for bands and emerging artists. I wasn't certain about it, but he always seemed to have the knack for picking out trends that would work.

As for Pete, things didn't go well for him.

After a few weeks in hospital, he was taken to prison. While there was a definite case against him for Harry, he never admitted how many women he had killed on his travels nor how he'd managed to find Amelia and what had happened to her before her body turned up in the lake. He confessed to his role in moving Kaja's body but was unable to provide a meaningful description of the man in the red van who'd triggered his obsession. He was shown pictures of that enigmatic figure with his beard and the red van and had gazed with some interest at them before feigning ignorance.

There were many other charges, too, including the ones Leila had made, but pinning the suspected murders on him of the missing women across Europe proved to be harder. His carefully woven trail of misdirection and cover-ups had been effective, concealing his acts from immediate detection. Over the years, he'd perfected those skills.

He had offered to show the Spanish authorities where he'd hidden bodies, although it was suspected that he was planning to escape while in the country. It took time to arrange but he was finally able to leave England under heavy guard, which he did so while covering his face with his long coat and hat, arms pinned to his sides. He was moved to a vehicle from a side door to the prison so that any journalists hanging around outside would miss him.

In Spain, his police escort failed to prevent the brother of one of the missing women from shooting him twice in the head, right through his hat, a hat that miraculously stayed on even as he fell to the ground, leaking his terrible memories and psychopathy through the damaged felt and onto the road in a pool of blood.

The Lady in the Lake had been found; Kaja was finally put to rest and the band had broken up forever.

For a time, we'd been five friends. An introvert, an extrovert, a charmer, a composer and... me.

The headlines went silent again, just the way I preferred it.

THE END

ABOUT THE AUTHOR

Scott Dunlop

Scott Dunlop was born in Scotland, spending a large part of his childhood in England before moving with his parents to Cape Town, South Africa. He grew up in what he calls "a city with two faces", referring to both its intense beauty and the dichotomy of its resources.

He's the father of three and has spent his adult life as a bookseller and then as a professional journalist, writer, and communicator. He feels that life is best understood through words, art, and music and is annoyed that he's never mastered any of those three disciplines.

He plays guitar and ukulele and once sang in a punk band so bad they were paid not to play.

He currently lives and works in Malta.